PUFFIN BOOKS

THE ROOT CELLAR

Imagine climbing down the steps of an abandoned root cellar – and finding yourself suddenly transported into the world of a hundred years ago . . .

Imagine meeting a boy and a girl who are part of that world, making friends with them, and getting caught up with them in the excitement and chaos of the American Civil War across the border . . .

This is what happens to Rose Larkin. Rose is an orphan who lives in New York City. But when she is twelve years old, she is packed off to live with relatives in an old farmhouse in Ontario. She is lonely and unhappy . . . until one day she discovers the old root cellar – and stumbles into the world of the late 1860s.

There Rose makes friends with Will and Susan, and when Will runs away to fight and does not return, she realizes she must reach across time to help save him. She and Susan set out on a journey that brings them into unexpected dangers and adventures – a journey on which Rose gains the strength and confidence to deal with her own world.

Janet Lunn was born in Texas and raised in New England. She has lived in Canada since 1946. She is married and has five children and three grandchildren. She is a leading children's book critic and reviewer, and has lectured extensively on the subject.

Another book by Janet Lunn
DOUBLE SPELL

THE
ROOT
CELLAR

Janet Lunn

PUFFIN BOOKS

PUFFIN BOOKS

Published by the Penguin Group
27 Wrights Lane, London W8 5TZ, England
Viking Penguin Inc., 40 West 23rd Street, New York, New York 10010, USA
Penguin Books Australia Ltd, Ringwood, Victoria, Australia
Penguin Books Canada Ltd, 2801 John Street, Markham, Ontario, Canada L3R 1B4
Penguin Books (NZ) Ltd, 182–190 Wairau Road, Auckland 10, New Zealand

Penguin Books Ltd, Registered Offices: Harmondsworth, Middlesex, England

First published in Canada by Lester & Orpen Dennys 1981
First published in the United States by Charles Scribner's Sons 1983
Published in Puffin Books 1983
Reprinted 1983, 1985 (twice), 1986, 1987, 1988

Illustrations by N. R. Jackson

Printed and bound in Great Britain by
Cox & Wyman Ltd, Reading
Typeset in Sabon

Library of Congress Catalog Card No: 84-13195

CONTENTS

To Richard, who has always known the
island and the bay, this book is lovingly
dedicated.

With grateful acknowledgements to the Ontario Arts
Council, and to the Canada Council for providing the
travel grant that enabled me to research this book in
Ontario, Oswego, New York, Washington and
Richmond. And particular thanks to my son John,
who wrote Will's song for him.

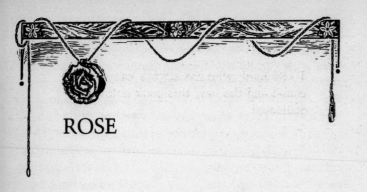

ROSE

It was a cold wet afternoon in October when Rose Larkin came to live in the house at Hawthorn Bay. Rain dripped from the branches of the big horse-chestnut tree in the front yard and hung in large drops from the tangle of bushes around the house. Rose stood in the driveway, where Aunt Stella had left her, feeling that she had never been in a place more dismal in all her life. Its bleakness seemed to echo her own sense of being completely abandoned. In the weeks since the death of her grandmother she had been shipped from relative to relative and finally delivered — like a package, she thought bitterly — to an aunt and uncle she had never seen.

Rose was an orphan. Her mother and father had been killed in a car crash when she was three years old, and she had gone to live with her mother's mother in New York City. Her grandmother was a business woman who travelled all over the world. An austere woman, more dutiful than loving, she took Rose with her everywhere she went which meant that Rose spent as much time in hotels as she did in their apartment on Upper Fifth Avenue in New York.

Grandmother did not believe in schools. "They teach only what's fashionable — and that not very well," she snorted. So every evening, from the day Rose was five, they did lessons together. Every morning she had to do homework. Every afternoon she was free to do as she pleased. Wet days she read or explored the hotel. Fine days she poked around shops or went to museums or movies in foreign languages. She often sat for hours in parks, watching people — old people feeding the birds, shoppers, strollers, mothers or fathers with their children. Rose had never known other children and they fascinated her. She often longed to speak to them, sometimes even to become part of their games, but they frightened her. They were apt to be rough and make loud jokes, and she was afraid she wouldn't know what to say to them. Her grandmother told her more than once that she was better off without them, that she would learn more about being an adult if she associated only with adults.

In consequence she didn't know much about living with people. She and her grandmother were like two polite strangers together. Rose had learned early that when she was quiet and obedient her grandmother was pleasant — and not so pleasant when she wasn't. The death of her parents had left her with a nagging fear that her grandmother too might disappear if she misbehaved so she became a stiff, self-possessed child about whom many said she was more like a china doll than a little girl. She didn't look like a china doll. Her bright red hair was pulled tightly into two neat braids. She had a long nose and her face was pointed which gave her a slightly elfish look and sometimes led strangers to expect mischief or humour until they looked more closely at her set chin, her mouth so firmly shut and the guarded expression that was too often in her large grey eyes.

Without other children, an alien among adults, Rose came to the conclusion when she was about eight that she didn't belong in the world. She believed she was a creature from somewhere else. She could no longer remember her mother or father and she figured that the story about her having parents was made up to keep her from finding the truth. She hadn't the least idea where she might have come from but she had absolute faith that one day she would go there. Meanwhile she did her best to mind her own business and keep out of everyone's way. She was often lonely but she had early accepted loneliness as a condition of her life.

The year Rose turned twelve, her grandmother decided she should go to boarding school in Paris. They went to Paris together and the first night, in their hotel room, her grandmother had a heart attack. Rose was paralyzed with fear.

"Don't stand there gaping, child," her grandmother croaked between gasps of pain. "Call the desk. Get a doctor." Feeling as though her feet were made of lead, like someone in a nightmare, Rose did as she was told, and she went along in the ambulance to the hospital and sat in the waiting room while her grandmother was wheeled off on a stretcher. She forced herself to think of nothing while doctors and nurses bustled around her. Half an hour later the doctor came to tell her that her grandmother had died.

Stunned, she managed a polite nod and said stiffly, "Merci, Monsieur." She took a taxi back to the hotel,

phoned Great-Aunt Millicent in New York and waited
for Great-Uncle Arnold to come on the night plane. Her
hands shook and she had no appetite but otherwise she
managed to remain calm and possessed all through the
trip home and the funeral afterwards.

She spent a week with each of her grandmother's
sisters after which they had a meeting in Great-Aunt
Millicent's apartment. Rose sat rigidly on the edge of
her chair. Uncle Arnold said he thought she ought to be
sent to school, Aunt Millicent said she wasn't sure what
should be done, and Aunt Stella said, ''Why not send
her to Nan Henry's?''

Nan Henry was Rose's father's only sister. She lived
with her husband and four sons on an island off the
north shore of Lake Ontario. When Aunt Stella phoned
her, Nan said, as if it was the simplest thing in the
world, ''Of course Rose can come and live with us. Tell
her to bring a bucket of paint and a paint brush, we've
just moved in.'' At which, when Aunt Stella reported
the words, Aunt Millicent raised her eyes towards the
ceiling but offered no argument.

''Now, dear,'' she gushed, ''before you go to your new
home, I think we'd better do something about you,
hadn't we?'' Rose felt like a specimen in a museum case
as Aunt Millicent gave her braids a small tug, patted the
lace collar of her good navy blue challis dress and ap-
praised her with sharp eyes but she was much too
bewildered and too well behaved to say anything. She
went obediently to the hairdresser where, with two
quick chops, her braids were left lying on the floor and
her hair was in inch-long curls all over her head. ''So
chic,'' twittered Aunt Millicent and took Rose from

there to a shop where she bought her a pair of tight black velvet pants, a pair of tall slim boots with two-inch heels and a sealskin jacket, clothes suited to a seventeen- or eighteen-year-old fashion model. On Rose they looked foolish and she was thoroughly miserable in them. And she felt naked without her braids.

Aunt Stella, who worked in television, said she had a trip to Toronto coming up and wouldn't mind making a bit of a detour to drop Rose off at the Henrys'. So one night in October Uncle Arnold packed all Rose's belongings into the back of Aunt Stella's blue sports car and before dawn the next morning Rose and Aunt Stella left New York.

Rose sat most of the day with her fists clenched in her lap, alternately chafing at the discomfort of her new clothes and shorn hair and thinking of the dreadful things that were sure to happen in the Henry household. "Who is Aunt Nan, anyway?" she wondered peevishly, and the answer came, "A woman with no sense." Her grandmother had said that once when Rose had asked. What did that mean anyway? And then there were the boys — four of them. She shuddered. The day wore on. The New York State Thruway was endless, but at the same time it wasn't long enough. Rose would have been glad as they came nearer and nearer to the Canadian border if they could have driven for ever. By the time they reached Lake Ontario she had worked herself into a frenzy of worry. When Aunt Stella drove onto the little ferry that would take them to the island and said, "We should be there in not more than half an hour," Rose was almost ready to leap out of the car.

It had been raining on the island but even with

everything grey and wet and most of the leaves gone from the trees the low, rolling countryside was pretty. There were big old houses and barns, huge silos and field after field of bright orange pumpkins, making a kind of space Rose wasn't used to. And there were not many people in sight. In cities there were always people.

They passed through several small, neat villages, with big houses of brick or clapboard where late flowers bloomed along porches and walks. Eight miles past the last village, near the south shore of the island, Aunt Stella turned down a dirt road. It curved around a deep bay — *Hawthorn Bay* a sign read. Aunt Stella had her hand-drawn map on her lap and she told Rose to start looking at mail boxes. They had driven around a sharp corner and over a creek when they came to an old red brick house, sadly neglected and all but surrounded by bushes. An enormous horse-chestnut tree in the front yard loomed over it, and a pair of gnarled maples leaned towards each other out by the road. The name HENRY was printed in uneven letters on the rusty mail box.

Aunt Stella pulled into the driveway and stopped. "I can see why Nan said bring a bucket of paint," she said wryly. She got out of the car. "You wait here. I'll tell them we've arrived."

Rose watched as she picked her way through the tall grass and weeds in her high-heeled shoes and knocked on the front door. No answer. She went across to the smaller door at the west end of the house and knocked. No answer. She pushed open the door and went inside. In less than two minutes she was back.

"There's nobody home. Isn't that like Nan. I'll bet

she's got the wrong day. Damn! Well, there's a note on the kitchen table saying, 'Dear furnace man, we'll be back soon, come in and go right down to the cellar.' How she expects him to find the note unless he's already in I can't imagine, and anyway who leaves notes to the furnace man saying, 'dear furnace man'? Listen Rose, I really can't wait. I'm sorry to just dump you like this but I expected Nan to be here and I promised this guy I'd be in Toronto for dinner. I'm sure you'll be O.K. because the note says they'll be right back. Why don't you make yourself at home. Now, if you'll give me a hand with this stuff ——''

"I'm not going to stay here," declared Rose. It was the first time she could remember ever having voiced an objection to anything she had been told to do but the prospect of living in a derelict house remote from anything or anyone she'd ever known filled her with sudden panic. She didn't plead, she stated flatly, "I'll come with you to Toronto. You won't find me any trouble. Then I'll go back to New York. I'll go to school there."

"Don't be silly, Rose." Aunt Stella stopped hauling suitcases out of the trunk and brushed a wet leaf from her suit. "This is just the thing for you though you may not think so right now. I expect you're missing your grandmother but Nan's a good sort and the boys are just what you need. You'll love it here. Now come along and give me a hand."

Rose gave up. That one small declaration of independence was all she could manage. Mechanically, she grabbed a suitcase. Together she and Aunt Stella tugged and lugged and got the three big suitcases and two boxes of books out of the car and into the dark house. They didn't stay long, just long enough for Rose to get an impression of a low-ceilinged, old-fashioned kitchen full of books and papers and dirty dishes. Back to the car to make sure there was nothing of Rose's left there and then Aunt Stella was off.

"Goodbye, Rose, I'm sure you're going to love it here! Be a good girl, have fun. Tell Nan I'm sorry I missed her." With a quick wave, she was off down the road leaving Rose standing in the driveway clutching her overnight bag.

She stood there uncertainly. She didn't want to go back inside and she couldn't stand in the driveway all afternoon. She stared numbly at the house.

It was a big, square house with a low wing at either end. There had clearly been a porch all along the front. Where it had been attached there was a smudged line spotted with bricks of the wrong size and colour, mortared in to repair holes. The chimney at the east end had crumbled and the roof of the shed that still clung to the kitchen was badly caved in.

"Nobody cares about this house," thought Rose. "Nobody." Suddenly, and without the sun actually coming out, the sky brightened to a luminous silver and the old house stood etched on the surrounding air as though it had appeared from some other time or place. It looked like a painting, with its bright red bricks, its white trim, its pink and blue and purple flower beds. From somewhere near came the sound of water gurgling and a bird cried out a single note that echoed and re-echoed in the silence.

Rose gasped and took an eager step forward. The

brightness faded. The sky grew grey again. The moment was past. The house was as it had been, its bricks darkened with age and rain, its trim all but peeled off — and there were no flowerbeds.

"I don't understand that." Rose shivered inside her fur coat. Still holding tightly to her overnight bag she marched resolutely up to the front door. Close up it was shabbier and more pathetic than at a distance. In front of the door there was an old pump she had not noticed before, and the ground around it was bare mud.

Grabbing hold of the pump handle for support, Rose leaned forward and peered into the nearest downstairs front window. From inside two bright black eyes peered back at her.

For a full second Rose stood frozen, her heart beating frantically. She did not notice that her overnight bag had slipped from her hand. She leaned against the pump handle, and as the shock wore off she could see that the eyes were not floating in space — they belonged in a small, sun-browned face as wrinkled as an apple doll's. The mouth was turned up at the edges and the nose was so small it almost disappeared into the wrinkles. The eyes were like dark moons, blinking and staring at Rose in obvious disbelief. As Rose stared through the window, the whole face crinkled up in a smile so bright it seemed as if the sun had come out. Then it disappeared.

In an instant, an old woman appeared from around the corner of the house. She was small, not much taller than Rose. On top of her apple-doll face, her white hair, the colour of old ivory, was neatly wound around her head in two thin braids. She was dressed in a cotton print dress that reached almost to her ankles, with a flowered apron over it and a large knitted grey shawl around her shoulders. She was the oddest-looking person Rose had ever seen.

"I see you come back." The old woman smiled. "I didn't mean to scare you." Shyly she reached out and touched Rose on the arm. Rose jumped back nervously.

"I beg your pardon?"

"You come back."

"I beg your pardon. I think you must have made a mistake. I've never been here before."

"Oh, Rose!" For a moment the old woman looked at her sadly. Then a light of understanding came to her eyes. "I see," she said slowly, "I see. You only just come now. Then you don't . . . of course you don't. Oh, Rose! Now *I* done it." She stopped and looked around her apprehensively.

"I suppose she must be senile," Rose decided, "like old Aunt Prue. In a minute she'll start shouting and throwing things." As she had been taught to do with her grandmother's aged aunt, she explained slowly and loudly that she was Rose Larkin from New York City.

"I've come to live with Aunt Nan and Uncle Bob. Are you a relative of theirs?"

The old woman sighed. She shrugged her shoulders uncomfortably. "Oh, well, I'm Mrs. Morrissay, that's who I am and —— oh, my sweet Hannah! What's happened to my house?" As she'd been talking, Mrs. Morrissay had turned towards the house. She walked up to the front door and poked her fingers through the broken panes of glass on either side. She stamped on the loose doorstep then walked slowly along the front of the house, patting the weathered window frames, thumping the ill-fitting bricks. She faced Rose. "It looks old and queer. It's all but a ruin. Rose, you go to do something!"

"Me?" Rose was so astonished she forgot her manners.

"Well, you . . . Lord's mercy! What's that?"

Rose whirled around. A large green station wagon was pulling into the driveway. Panic threatened again. "It's them," she whispered. "It's the Henrys, isn't it?" She turned back towards Mrs. Morrissay, instinctively seeking support, but the old woman was not there. As swiftly and as strangely as she had come, she had gone — without even a stirring in the bushes.

THE HOUSE
AT HAWTHORN BAY

They tumbled out of the station wagon and across the yard, four boys and a round untidy-looking woman carrying two large shopping bags, a potted geranium and, under one arm, a load of books.

Halfway across the yard Aunt Nan saw Rose. She stopped. The books slipped from under her arm. "Oh dear, never mind, are you looking for someone? Are —— oh my Lord, you must be Rose!" she cried. "Oh, good heavens, it's today! Isn't it tomorrow? Oh, dear!"

"Mother! I told you the letter said Monday." A tall, thin, long-legged boy was half bouncing, half dancing on first one foot then the other in front of his mother. "I told you. Now, if you'd listen to what I ——"

"Shut up, George. Mother you're losing the groceries." The second boy, not quite as tall and not nearly as wild looking, grabbed the bags of groceries and the geranium before they could follow the books to the ground. He turned to stare at Rose. Two small boys grabbed him by his arms and whispered loudly and urgently, "Is it Rose, Sam? Is it?"

"I don't know. Are you Rose?"

"Yes, I'm Rose," said Rose stiffly, feeling all their eyes on her, conscious of how ridiculous she must look in her city boots and pants and fur jacket, standing by the old pump, desperate for a place to hide. Wildly she thought of running, but her feet would not budge. "Aunt Stella couldn't stay," she blurted out.

"Oh, Rose!" Aunt Nan had got over her surprise. She rushed over and threw her arms around Rose and gave her a warm kiss.

Rose flinched as though she had been struck. No one, in her memory, had ever showed her more affection than Grandmother's occasional pats on the head and Aunt Millicent's showy little kisses in the air. Aunt Nan did not seem to notice. She went on talking. She was astounding, the way she looked and the way she talked. She was short, and as plump as an overstuffed cushion. She had a full mouth, warm brown eyes and a lot of soft brown hair coming undone from a knot at the back of her head. She had on a loose plaid dress with a big, bright green sweater over it, no stockings, and on her feet a pair of running shoes with holes in them. And she never stopped talking.

"How tiny you are," she crowed. "My goodness, I can hardly see you inside that coat. I write stories for girls. It's to get away from boys your uncle Bob says, so you can imagine how nice it's going to be to have you here. Of course the new one might be a girl." Aunt Nan patted her stomach and Rose realized that some of the plumpness was because Aunt Nan was expecting a baby.

"Not that I don't like boys." Aunt Nan's voice sounded like a xylophone going up and down the scales.

"I like my boys very much. Come and meet them. Imagine being this old and never knowing each other! Boys! Boys! Come and meet your cousin. Sam! George! Twins!"

The twins, dressed in identical jeans and dark blue sweaters, looked exactly like their mother with the same round faces, the same brown hair and round eyes. They inspected Rose solemnly from the protection of their mother's skirt.

"Jimmy and Brian are the babies. They're six. That's Sam, he's fourteen." Sam was crossing the yard with the fifth load of groceries. "Hello," he said, nodded curtly towards Rose and continued on his way. The only impression Rose had of him was that he was a big, stocky boy with bushy red hair.

"And that's George." Aunt Nan laughed. "George is fifteen. He talks a lot and thinks he knows everything."

George slammed the back of the station wagon shut with his foot and came loping towards them. He had light curly brown hair, blue eyes, a wide full mouth in a small round face. In his jeans and worn brown sweater, too short at the waist and wrists, he looked like a scarecrow.

"Hi," he said in a loud, croaking voice. "Hi. I knew you were coming today. You see I read the letter and ——"

"And that's all of us except Uncle Bob who had to go to a meeting this afternoon in Soames. He'll be back soon."

"How do you do?" said Rose.

"Mother!" George was exasperated. "Mother, you forgot to introduce Grim. You see, Rose, we have a cat called Grim for Grimalkin which means grey cat ——''

''Come on,'' said Aunt Nan. ''It's starting to rain again, and the wind's coming up. We'd better get your things inside, Rose, dear. Is that all you have, just that one little suitcase?''

''There are at least four thousand more in the kitchen,'' said George.

''Oh, good! Rose, where's Stella? How long have you been waiting for us out here in this wet yard?''

Rose explained that Aunt Stella had been in a hurry. She was going to mention meeting Mrs. Morrissay but Aunt Nan interrupted. ''Same old Stella. No time for anything. I swear someday she's going to drop dead in the middle of a TV show and when they go to pick up the body they'll find it's nothing but dust because she's forgotten to eat for three months.'' With one hand firmly on Rose's arm, Aunt Nan steered her through the kitchen door, talking all the while. ''Look at all those boxes! Oh, my goodness, child, I expect you left New York very early. You must be exhausted. Why don't I take you right up to your room? We only found out last week, of course, that you were coming, so we haven't had a chance to do much with it. Here, give me your suitcase. The boys can carry up the big ones.''

''No, thank you. I'll carry it.'' Rose held tightly to her overnight bag and followed Aunt Nan from the dark kitchen through another gloomy room and up a flight of steep stairs to a little room at the back of the house. Like the outside of the house, and the glimpse she had had of downstairs, the room was dismal. Its flowered wallpaper, dried and yellowed with age, was in shreds. The plaster had come away from half of one wall, and where the roof had leaked there was a large brown stain on the ceiling and running down the wall by the bed. She could see that the wide boards of the floor had once been painted dark red but the paint was almost gone and some of the boards had come loose. A brass bed stood against one wall. There was a small white dresser beside it. Opposite, next to the window, was a low desk also painted white. The room smelled musty and a little sour — Sam told Rose later he thought it was because of all the dead rats and mice in the walls.

"The dresser and the desk were mine when I was little," said Aunt Nan, "and the bed was here in the house when we came. Isn't it nice?"

Rose did not answer. She had never been anywhere, dreamed of any place uglier or more depressing than this one. As though in answer to her bitter thoughts, Aunt Nan sighed. "You probably think we're all crazy. People do, I guess. We're a bit disorganized but we've only been here a month. Your Uncle Bob was in the forces, and he's just retired. That's why we came down here. He's the game warden for the island, and this is all so much better for him we should have done it years ago. You know the house is one hundred and sixty years old — it's going to be beautiful when we get it fixed up and — oh Lord, Bob will be home any minute. I'd better get supper started. I'll leave you to settle yourself before supper. O.K.?" Without waiting for an answer she was off down the stairs, her burbling words punctuated by the excited whispers of the twins.

Then came Sam and George struggling with two heavy suitcases each, the twins right behind them.

"What's in these things? The Statue of Liberty? Haw! Haw!" George dropped the bags with a thump, tripped over Sam and went down for more. Sam put his down, said nothing, and turned to follow George. The twins scooted after. Up they came again until all the suitcases and boxes were piled around Rose who stood in the middle of the floor in an agony of shyness, willing them to be finished.

"Well," said George, "I guess that's done." Rose mumbled "thank you" but when she said nothing more, he cleared his throat, looked around, stared at her and said, "Well, see you later," and they were gone.

Rose closed the door after them as tightly as it would close. Still in her coat and boots, she sat on the edge of the bed. For a moment the chaos of the last weeks threatened to overwhelm her. One week she had been with her grandmother on her way to Paris, steeling herself to face boarding school, three days later she had been flying home with her grandmother lying dead in the baggage compartment. Three weeks more and she was in a run-down farmhouse in Canada surrounded by a family noisier, more rambunctious than any in her worst imaginings. She clamped her lips tightly shut and reached down and unzipped her overnight bag. It had in it her nightclothes in case she and Aunt Stella had had to stop at a motel, and her treasures: her music box and her mother's old copy of *The Secret Garden*. They had been hers since her parents died, and Rose had always carried them with her, feeling that without them, and the silver rose she wore on a chain around her neck, she wouldn't be any kind of person at all.

She became aware of a noise at her door. She looked up and saw the latch moving. She turned around quickly. "Who's there?"

The door was edged open and two pairs of brown eyes

peered through the opening at her. "It's us," whispered the twins.

"Yes?"

"Mother says it's supper time." They stood looking at her for a moment, let out a long sigh in unison and retreated from the door. Rose could hear them thumping rapidly down the stairs.

She took off her boots, rummaged through her suitcases, found her loafers and the plaid skirt she was used to wearing, and put them on. "I don't suppose I need to wash for dinner," she muttered, but all the same she found her hairbrush and swiftly brushed through her short curls.

On her way downstairs she passed the open doorway of the next room. She caught a glimpse of firelight and stopped to peek inside. To her astonishment a girl was busily pulling up the covers on a big, handsome four-poster bed. There was a small black stove with a bright fire between the windows, a round rag rug on the floor and a cheerful tidiness that wasn't anywhere else in the house. Hastily she backed out, puzzled, and went downstairs.

Downstairs was like turning on a radio and getting all the stations at once. The television was going in the living room. George was perched on one arm of the sofa making running comments as he watched. Aunt Nan was beating something with an electric beater in the kitchen and talking in a loud voice to someone who made an occasional rumbling response. In sing-song voices the twins were anxiously telling their mother, "We don't want any peas, we don't want any peas."

Rose stood at the foot of the stairs trying to take it all

in. The living room was in worse condition than her bedroom. It was a large room full of doors and windows, cluttered with furniture that appeared to have been left wherever the moving men had deposited it a month earlier. The bare lath was exposed through large holes in the walls. She couldn't understand why the front room upstairs had been made so charming while the living room was in such a state.

She went through into the kitchen which was much more cheerful. It had been scrubbed and repaired. Along one wall there was a big old fireplace with a bake oven beside it. The other walls and the low ceiling were a honey-coloured wood that reflected softly the light from the fire burning in the fireplace and from the lamps on the mantel and the small table under the front window. Against the back wall was a big brown electric range, counters (obviously new) and a sink with small square windows over it. There were shelves for dishes over the windows — but most of the dishes were on the big table in the middle of the room or piled up dirty in the sink. An old wooden rocking-chair stood by the front window, covered — as was every other possible space — with books, magazines, rubber boots and sweaters.

Something was burning. Aunt Nan pulled a smoking pot off the stove while she talked to a man with bushy black hair and a big black moustache, who sat on a high stool just out of her way. The twins were poking their fingers into various bowls and dishes until one of them happened to turn and see Rose standing in the doorway. "Here she is," he whispered and tugged at his father's hand. His twin echoed, "Here she is, she's here!"

Rose drew back a step. Her uncle Bob looked up. He

got up and walked over to her. "How do you do, Rose?"
He smiled and shook hands. "I'm glad you've come to
stay with us."

Uncle Bob was tall and thin like George, with those
same bright blue eyes, but Uncle Bob's had wrinkles at
the corners and a quiet dreaminess about them. His
nose was thin and long. He asked about her trip from
New York and said he was sorry about her grandmother
having died. Before she had to say anything, Nan called
out that supper was ready and they sat down to eat
burned spaghetti, peas and chopped cabbage salad.
There was orange pudding for dessert.

Sam and George sat opposite Rose. "Do you always
talk with that accent — awrange pudding?" George
brayed.

Rose flushed with embarrassment. "I've never
thought about it before," she said.

"Did your grandmother really die in Paris?"

"Yes."

"What did you do?"

"I'm used to Paris and they know me in that hotel. I
managed," said Rose coldly. She did not want to talk to
George. She did not want to talk about her grandmother
dying in Paris to anyone.

"Do you ——" George began.

"George!" Uncle Bob said sharply, "This is not a
court martial!" He turned apologetically to Rose. "I imagine you'll find mealtime here a bit different from what
you're used to."

"Grandmother and I generally ate in restaurants,"
replied Rose. She caught Sam looking at her, and in the
quick way he turned she had the feeling he was angry.

Aunt Nan kept up a steady flow of talk. The twins sat on either side of Rose and did not take their eyes from her face throughout the meal. Nobody mentioned the girl upstairs making the bed and nobody mentioned Mrs. Morrissay. Finally, when dinner was nearly over, Rose got up her courage and asked about the girl. For an answer she got six blank stares and a dead silence.

"I expect she's the maid," said Rose.

"The maid?" Aunt Nan put down her fork.

George let out a yell of laughter. "The maid! That's a good one!"

"Well, as she didn't come to dinner I thought. . . ."

"What are you talking about, dear? There's nobody upstairs. Are you playing a joke?" Aunt Nan smiled indulgently at Rose.

Rose did not answer. Everyone else was laughing. She flushed with embarrassment and anger. Why were they saying there was nobody upstairs? She had seen the girl. But she wasn't going to risk another bout of George's laughter or Sam's glowering so she said no more about it, and did not ask about Mrs. Morrissay either. Instead, she asked to be excused. In her primmest voice, she said, "I've had a rather busy day. I'd like to go to bed."

Uncle Bob said approvingly, "Good soldiers need their sleep," and George called after her, "Tell the maid we need her in the kitchen if you see her. Haw! Haw!"

Rose went swiftly but sedately upstairs and straight to the front room. There was no one there. There was no four-poster bed, no stove with a fire in it, no round rag rug. The room was cold and dark and as ramshackle as the rest of the house.

She was scared. She went to her own room, closed the

door and sat down on her bed with her coat over her. She wanted to be ready to run in case something horrible should happen.

"This place is very odd," she whispered into the dark night. "It's like that story about the girl who had the plague in a hotel and they took her away and nobody would say she'd ever been there. I saw a girl making that bed. I know I did. What happened to her? Why don't they want me to know about her? And I saw that old lady — nobody's said anything about her, and ——" She suddenly remembered the strange vision of the house. "I saw flowers. Delphiniums. I saw them."

She sat in the dark, silently huddled under her coat, listening to the wind rattle the loose window frame and whistle through the cracks. A tree scratched on the window. The room was cold and musty. Usually, talking to herself was a kind of comfort. It was almost like having a companion but on this night there was no comfort. She had a sudden sharp pang of loneliness for her grandmother. She did not deeply grieve for her — her grandmother had not let her come close enough for that — but she missed the comfort of their familiar relationship and the life they had known together. She ached to leave the frightening strangeness of people who were so noisy and unpredictable and whose house held in it people they pretended were not there. She choked back the tears that threatened, as she always had choked back tears, until her throat was sore, and she sat with her arms tight around her knees until she fell over fast asleep.

She was awakened hours later by a thought. "How did that old lady know my name? She talked to me as if she knew me."

Wide awake by now she sat up and listened to the quiet. It had stopped raining and the wind had died. She got up and went to the window. The clouds had gone from the sky. The moon was full. The night had washed away all colour and, outside, the world was a black and white and silver landscape.

The tall grass beyond the bushes was as soft and pale as doves' feathers. Here and there apple and thorn trees dotted the slope, their trunks and limbs twisted and black, a few late apples hanging on the boughs like tiny iridescent globes. A creek followed a meandering path to the bay, gleaming under the moon.

Down past the creek was a small wood and through it the bay was just visible, shining whitely through the trees. Up close to the house the bushes made a dark smudge. In their midst was a little glade, not much bigger in diameter than the height of a large apple tree, a circle of bright light in the dark.

Rose stared down at the glade as though hypnotized. Then she left the window, slid her feet into her shoes, opened her door and crept down the stairs, through the silent house and out into the night.

Outside she pushed her way through the dense tangle of the bushes. She emerged into the glade, scratched and out of breath. There was the creek, and beside it was a small hawthorn tree. Its bark was silvery, its delicate branches stretched out gracefully around it like a hundred arms, its twigs and branchlets forming an intricate tracery to which tiny pointed leaves and a few dark berries still clung.

The ground was covered with leaves from the hawthorn and from the lilac and chokecherry that surrounded the clearing. The creek bubbled swiftly over the stones and bits of old branches that lay clearly visible in its bed. It smelled of wet leaves and moss.

Rose had never seen any place so beautiful. She turned around slowly, absorbing it all. The glade was quite bare except for the creek and the little hawthorn tree, and an old cedar fence post close by, leaning over and half buried in dead leaves.

On an impulse she gathered a few small hawthorn branches from the ground, ones that still had leaves and a few clusters of berries, and put them into the hollow of the fence post.

"There," she whispered, "now I have a secret garden." Quietly she went back into the house and upstairs. This time she took off her clothes and got into bed — and slept soundly until morning.

GHOSTS

When Rose came into the kitchen the next morning she felt as though she had stepped into a fairytale at the exact moment a spell had been cast. Uncle Bob had his coffee mug halfway to his mouth. George and Aunt Nan had stopped talking. The twins had stopped eating. Everyone was staring at Sam.

As Rose came though the door they began. Aunt Nan's voice was the loudest and most excited. "Why didn't you say something? Oh, Sam!" she wailed.

"Come off it, Sam." George was disgusted, and Uncle Bob scolded. "Now Sam you know that's impossible." The twins, looking at Sam with awe, began chanting, "Sam saw a ghost, Sam saw a ghost!"

"Tell me exactly what it looked like," demanded Aunt Nan. "Well," Sam began slowly, pushing his hand through his thick hair, his blunt face puckered in a half-embarrassed grimace, "it was like an old lady with a shawl on. At first she was just a shadow, I mean, not a shadow but one of those things you make when you put your hand behind a sheet with a light on it and make your hand look like a rabbit or something. You just see the shape. It ——"

"It's a silhouette, Sam, a silhouette," George interrupted. "It's named after Etienne de Silhouette in the eighteenth century. He ——"

"O.K., a silhouette, and it walked through that door," Sam pointed towards the doorway where Rose was standing. Involuntarily she jumped back. George laughed.

"Good morning, Rose." Aunt Nan smiled broadly. "Go on, Sam. You said the silhouette came in. What happened to it?"

"Well, it leaned over as if it meant to put something on the table then it disappeared. That's all."

"That's all." Aunt Nan sighed happily. "And that's what I'll talk about. I've promised to go to Toronto today and talk about my books to some kids in a library and I'm going to talk about Sammy's ghost. Oh, why didn't I see it? I think I'll write a book about Sam's ghost. Do you think I could call it that?"

"No." Sam got up from the table. "Anyway I don't think it really was a ghost. I think it was probably just shadows. This room is full of shadows. Shadows all over the place. They just look like ghosts. Here's the school bus." He picked up his books and his windbreaker and fled through the door. George was right behind him, and the twins crying, "Wait for us! Wait for us!" trotted after swinging their lunch boxes.

Aunt Nan got up from the table. "I completely forgot to tell you, Rose. I promised way last month I'd do this talk. I'm afraid you'll have to look after yourself today. I really am sorry. Later in the week we can go down and talk to the school. I expect you can find your own breakfast. Oh dear, I really am sorry — just leave the dishes. Have a good exploring time, oh dear, I have to run. Coming, Bob? I have to get that eight-thirty bus or I'm a cooked goose.''

Aunt Nan bustled out the door, the collar of her blouse awry, her hair already falling out of its bun. Uncle Bob followed, stopping long enough to say, ''I'll be home around four-thirty. Have a nice day, Rose. There are horses up the road and cows. The woods are full of small animals — go take a look.''

Two car doors slammed, there was the sound of the engine starting and the station wagon took off down the road. Silence.

Rose sat down at the table and stared at the breakfast debris without really seeing it. She had wanted to ask Aunt Nan some questions, questions about things she had to know, like what should she get for breakfast? Where was the front door key? What should she do if strangers came?

A tap dripped. The wind rattled an upstairs window. A stair creaked. ''There aren't ghosts,'' she told herself firmly. ''Sam was right, it was shadows. Ghosts are made up for books and movies. They don't exist.'' Unbidden, the image of the girl in the upstairs bedroom flashed in her mind. A ghost? Was that why everybody had laughed? They really did not know she was there? ''Impossible,'' she said aloud, her eyes darting around the room. ''It was shadows.''

Silence fell once more. Under the table the cat made a chirruping sound in his throat and jumped up onto Rose's lap. She screamed. Then she laughed shakily and began to scratch him behind his ears. She liked cats. Over the years she had befriended many hotel and alley cats. This cat was big and soft and grey. "Grimalkin is a good name for you," Rose told him. "Lots of fairytale cats are called Grimalkin. I wonder how the Henrys found that out." He put his head down, closed his eyes and began to purr.

There was nothing left to eat on the table but toast crumbs. Rose got up and searched the cupboards. She found a box of shredded wheat but there was no milk. She sat down again, crushing a dry shredded wheat biscuit, staring glumly at the chair where Sam had sat. She had never felt so completely without comfort.

Suddenly she remembered waking in the night and finding the glade in the bushes. She leaped to her feet and ran outside, half afraid she would discover that it had been no more real than the girl in the upstairs room.

The backyard in the morning was full of red and yellow and brown leaves blowing in the fresh wind. Rose pushed her way through the bushes and there, where she had remembered it, was the glade, and in the hollow fence post she found the bouquet of leaves and berries she had put there in the night.

She sighed with relief. "It's a good secret." She picked up Grimalkin who had followed her and carried him back to the house.

For one frightening second as she opened the door she thought she saw old Mrs. Morrissay in the corner of the room but when she looked again there was no one there.

"This room *is* full of shadows," she said loudly as if to dispel them by the strength of her voice. Nervously she set about exploring the house, partly from curiosity, partly because she wanted to make sure there were no ghosts anywhere.

The rooms were all depressingly alike in their need of

repair. The bedroom over the kitchen, obviously Sam's and George's, was full of electrical paraphernalia, half-played games, paints, and an easel set up by the window.

Aunt Nan's workroom off the living room was so full of books and papers that Rose could not imagine being able to write in it. Aunt Nan's and Uncle Bob's bedroom at the other end of the house looked as though it might be beautiful if it were put to rights for it was big and sunny. Upstairs, over the living room, was her own room and the other where the girl had been making the bed. It was where the twins slept.

She looked that room over very carefully and could find nothing in its clutter of clothes and toys and electric trains to suggest what she had seen the evening before. She began to make it tidy, not because she was anxious to please the twins but because she felt that by making her own order there the room would be less likely to change itself into some other room. She folded the clothes, made the beds, put the toys and books in the big wooden box under the window. Then she made the train tracks into an elaborate pattern and set the train on it. She found the electric cord and, by the time she was really hungry, she realized the morning was over and she had spent it playing with six-year-olds' toy trains. Uncharacteristically, she giggled. "They don't have to know," she told Grimalkin.

As she came through the kitchen door she was certain she saw Mrs. Morrissay standing by the stove, but when she stepped forward there was no one there.

"I'm sure I saw . . ." Rose began, and stopped. On the table was a basket of eggs. "She *was* here! But where did she go?"

She ran to the back door and looked out. No one. "Very odd," she said nervously, "very odd."

She found some cheese in the refrigerator and shared it with the cat. Then she went outside again. She followed the creek down to the shore and stood for a while watching it empty into the bay in bubbles of white froth, the tall weeds below the water's surface bending under the pressure. She wandered through the woods and into the field that lay to the west and amused herself for a time identifying the trees before making her way back to the glade. It drew her. It wasn't only that it was beautiful. She had the feeling, standing with her back to the thorn tree, that something was expected of her here.

She was still standing there when she heard brakes screech in the driveway. The school bus had arrived. Rose ran back inside and fled up the stairs. She heard the door burst open downstairs letting in loud voices. Doors opened, doors closed, a shrill voice cried, "George, give me my toast." There was the sound of feet pounding on the stairs, whispers, then, "Jimmy! Someone's fixed up our train!" More whispers, the buzz of the electric train. Silence. The creak of Rose's door. The twins round faces appeared from behind it.

"Can we come in?"

"I suppose so."

"Did you fix our train?"

"Yes."

"Do you want to come and play with us?" asked one and the other added quickly, "You can have some of our toast."

"No, thank you. I have to put my things away."

"Can we watch?"

Rose looked at their eager faces and some of her stiffness softened. "All right." So while the twins watched and gave her a running commentary on their school and their family, Rose put her clothes away in the closet and drawers. The twins told her that Sam wasn't going to Italy, that George was a pig because he wouldn't share his chocolate bars, that their father liked to go fishing and that they liked hamburgers better than macaroni and cheese.

"Are we having macaroni and cheese for dinner?" asked Brian (or maybe it was Jimmy).

"Here's Daddy," said the other. Rose heard Uncle Bob's rumbling voice downstairs. Reluctantly she followed the twins. Uncle Bob was saying, "Oh, good. I didn't remember we had eggs. That's what we'll cook, eh?" Talk between Sam and George ceased abruptly as she entered the kitchen. She felt acutely uncomfortable.

That night, after Aunt Nan had come home and the twins had gone to bed, Rose settled down in bed to read with the cat beside her. After a while she became aware of Aunt Nan's voice from downstairs. "Sam," she was saying, "I know how disappointment can hurt but your attitude isn't helping to make that orphan child feel any better. I don't want to hear another word!"

"I don't care," Sam rumbled (not as deeply but in almost the same voice as Uncle Bob). "She doesn't do anything to make us feel good either. She's snooty. She's a snob. 'I'm used to Paris, they know me in that hotel.' " Sam imitated perfectly Rose's icy tones. "She goes around in her stupid fur coat glaring at people. She looks like a stuffed owl with pink hair!"

"Sam, you're most unkind. Rose has had a hard time. She's probably shy. She's lived a very funny life. It's true she's very prim, but I suppose her grandmother had something to do with that. And Rose's hair isn't pink, it's the same colour as yours. Your Uncle David had hair that colour."

"No, it isn't — mine's red. Hers is pink like the colour things get in the fridge when you leave them too long. I wish she'd take her mouldy, pink hair and her fur coat — doesn't she know you shouldn't skin animals — and go back to New York!"

"Sam!" Aunt Nan said sharply, "that's enough! You're fifteen years old. I know it's been hard for you but I think you might ——" A door slammed. In a moment it was opened again and Rose heard Aunt Nan's voice, more faintly: "Honestly, Bob, I think Sam is behaving . . . ." The door closed.

Rose was shattered. She had never heard herself attacked like that before. Snooty. Snob. What did he mean? And her hair wasn't pink! She got up and turned on the light and went to look at herself in the round mirror that hung over the dresser. She pulled furiously at the hated short ends of her red hair. What had she done to make him say things like that? She lay awake most of the night, cold and shaking, saying Sam's unkind words over and over to herself.

The next morning she stuffed the fur coat, and the boots, and the black velvet pants, into the back of her closet, and tied a large kerchief around her head. She could not look at Sam. Every time he came into the room she stiffened. She felt exposed, defenseless. She did the chores Aunt Nan set for her in silence and she spent most of the time in the next two days huddled in her thin sweater with her back against the hawthorn tree in the glade, finding comfort in the creek's soft gurgle as it flowed over the sticks and stones.

On Thursday Aunt Nan took her to school in Soames and talked to Mr. Hodgins, the principal, who wrinkled up his face and coughed a dry little cough at the news that Rose had never been to school.

"I don't believe we've ever had a problem like this before."

"You could give her a test couldn't you and find out how much she knows? I'm sure Rose isn't stupid."

"Yes, yes, I was going to suggest that, Mrs. Henry." Rose thought, "No he wasn't. He's a fool," but she sat down obediently and read a simple story out loud, wrote a couple of paragraphs about it, did some arithmetic problems, spelled a short list of words and answered a few questions about geography.

"Amazing." Mr. Hodgins coughed his dry little cough twice. "Your grandmother must have been a fine teacher."

"Yes."

"Well!" Mr. Hodgins was clearly a bit taken aback by her ready agreement. "You can probably go right into grade eight without any trouble."

Aunt Nan took Rose to the local dry-goods store afterwards. "You can't wear those good skirts all the time," she said and bought two pairs of jeans, a couple of T-shirts, a jacket and a pair of running shoes. Rose put on her new clothes the minute they got home. With her kerchief tied securely around her head she felt, if not comfortable, less conspicuous.

First thing Saturday morning the phone rang. It was a girl from Toronto to ask if she and her mother could drive out to see the ghost. Aunt Nan had said to all the children on Tuesday, "You must come and visit," but she had never expected that any of them would. "Come, of course," she told the girl and she said it to three others who called that day. It was like a constant parade of sightseers all entranced by the "weird" place where Nan Henry wrote her books. One girl asked Rose admiringly if she was Emily of Shadow Brook Farm, to which Rose replied frostily, "My name is not Emily and this, thank heaven, is the first time in my life I've ever been near a farm."

That evening as she was setting the table, and the last visitor was pulling out of the driveway, she muttered angrily to herself, "This place is like a zoo. Next time someone comes I'm going to jump up and down and ask for a banana." She turned to see Sam standing in the doorway, grinning. "Don't laugh at me!" she hissed. She was horrified to realize there were tears in her eyes. "You and your stupid ghosts! You made all those people come! I don't care if you hate me! I don't care if you think my hair is pink! I don't care if you think I'm a snob! Just don't you dare laugh at me!" She threw down the silverware with a clatter and ran from the room.

She stood with her back against the closed door of her bedroom until her quivering rage had subsided. Then she sat down at the desk in a cold calm, took out a sheet of the monogrammed paper her grandmother had given her at Christmas, and wrote Aunt Millicent a letter.

Dear Aunt Millicent,

I'm sure you didn't realize when you sent me here that the Henrys are all mad. Their house is falling apart. It's dirty. And they see ghosts. I want to come back to New York. I will go to school. I will go to an orphanage if you wish. I will go any place but here.

Your affectionate niece,
Rose Larkin

She looked up to reach for an envelope and there was Mrs. Morrissay coming towards her through the wall from the twins' room.

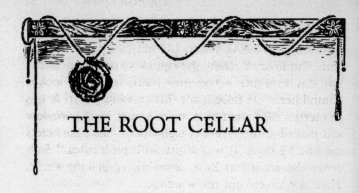

THE ROOT CELLAR

"Mrs. Morrissay!" A shudder like an electric shock ran through Rose. "What are you doing?" she whispered.

Mrs. Morrissay said nothing. She didn't move. She stood half in the twins' room, half in Rose's, a blue and orange kerchief tied around her head, a dust mop in her hand, looking very ill at ease.

Rose was trembling. Her hands were wet with cold sweat and she could hardly focus her eyes. Mrs. Morrissay came the rest of the way through the wall and into the room. She was no longer half visible. She was solid, three dimensional.

"You're Sam's ghost." Rose heard her own voice, strange and shrill and accusing.

"I ain't no ghost." Mrs. Morrissay was indignant. "I'm just plain myself, minding my own business and it happens."

"Happens?"

"I shift!"

"Shift?"

"Shift. I'm going along minding my own business like I said, hoeing or scrubbing or mopping, and right in the middle I shift. And you needn't be so cross, Rose. You ought to know better. It's not easy for a body to shift. I'm in my kitchen, then quick's a cow's tail after a fly, I'm in yours — or your bedroom." She looked around her. "Oh Rose, ain't this an awful sight? It was so pretty." She went over to the corner by the window and picked at the layers of wallpaper. "See, this here's the one I put up. It was white with pink roses." Suddenly she smiled at Rose, a warm, embracing smile. Then she looked out the window.

"Ain't it something how them bushes is all grown over. Funny how you can still see where the old garden was."

"Mrs. Morrissay, you have no right to be here!" Rose could barely control her shaking voice. Her sense of how things ought to be had never been so disturbed, not even by her grandmother's death. "You don't belong here, Mrs. Morrissay ——" Rose stopped abruptly, her fear, and her shock, subsiding before Mrs. Morrissay's smile. "I suppose it *is* your home?"

"Of course it's my house. I grew up in it. I was married in it. I'm like to die in it and" — Mrs. Morrissay finished with a sigh — "it seems I shift in it."

She reached over and took Rose's hand. Rose snatched it away. "It's all right," said Mrs. Morrissay soothingly. "Rose, I told you, I ain't no ghost. I ain't dead. I'm just shifted, and I don't know how no more than you do. It just happens, like I said. All I know is that if the good Lord sees fit to shift me, I shift. I suppose it's . . . well, I dunno. But I do belong here, and Rose I want you to make things right in my house for me."

"Mrs. Morrissay, I can't fix your house. It isn't my

house and anyway I don't even like this house. I'm not going to stay here. I'm going back to New York.''

Rose realized that she was actually talking to the old woman as easily as she had used her name, Mrs. Morrissay. ''How do you know so much about me? Who are you?''

But Mrs. Morrissay was staring at Rose in alarm. As if she hadn't heard her question, she said, ''Don't talk about going off like that, Rose. You ain't going to New York, you know you ain't —— oh!'' Mrs. Morrissay looked at Rose in alarm, opened her mouth to say something and disappeared, not slowly the way she had come but instantly, like a light being turned off.

Rose started back. Fearfully she put her hand towards the spot where Mrs. Morrissay had been standing. There was no one, nothing. Her mind was in a turmoil. At that moment, through the window, she caught sight of something blue and orange moving across the glade.

''There she is!'' Rose spoke aloud in her excitement. ''There's her kerchief!''

She flew down the stairs and out of the house. But there was no sign of Mrs. Morrissay in the clearing. Rose slumped down against the little hawthorn tree. ''It's true what I wrote Aunt Millicent,'' she whispered. ''They are mad. And now I think I must be mad too.''

She sat there, dejectedly scuffing the leaves with her feet, her mind going over and over what had happened. Her toe struck something metal. Surprised, she sat up straight and pushed at it with her foot. It clinked. She went over on her hands and knees to look. She brushed away the leaves and discovered that there were boards underneath with a metal latch of some sort.

"It's a door, a door in the ground, how odd." Excitedly she began to pull at the vines and thick grass that had grown over the boards, and when she had pulled most of them away she saw that, indeed, it was a door, two doors in fact with rusty hook-and-eye latches that secured them together. With much pulling and wrenching she managed to loosen them and slowly, slowly, with a great deal of straining and heaving she pried them open.

There were steps inside that had been made by cutting away the earth and laying boards across. The boards had all but rotted away but the earth steps were still there. At the bottom, facing her about three feet away, was another door, upright, also fastened with a hook-and-eye latch. The doorway was so low she had to stoop to get through.

Inside she found herself in a kind of closet with shelves along the sides on which stood crockery jars and glass sealers. On the floor stood several barrels with lids on them. The place was cold and damp but it looked to be in use.

"I don't understand. If Aunt Nan keeps her pickles and things here, why is it so hard to get into?" she thought. She had lifted the lid off one of the crocks and found it full of beets. Another was full of cucumber pickles. She looked up. Someone behind her was blocking the light. Quickly she turned around.

A girl, smaller but probably about the same age as her, stood at the top of the steps with a jar in her hands. It was the girl from the bedroom with the four-poster bed. She wore quite a long dress made of some rough dark brown material, with a white apron over it. On her feet

she had awkward-looking ankle-high boots. She had
dark brown hair in one long braid down her back, a plain
round freckled face, a small nose, a wide mouth — and
bright black eyes. They were blinking at Rose in consternation.

"Where'd you come from?" she demanded.

"I . . . I . . . what?"

"You'd best get out of our root cellar." The girl came
down the steps. "Missus will be terrible cross." She
reached up to the top shelf and brought down one of the
crocks. All the while she kept turning around to stare
nervously at Rose.

Rose stared back.

"You'd best come along now." The girl frowned.
"Honest, Missus don't like having strangers around."
She started back up the steps.

"Look" — Rose followed the girl — "look, isn't this
——" She'd been going to ask, "Isn't this Aunt Nan's
root cellar?" but the words never got spoken. At the top
of the steps she found herself standing beside a little
garden with rows of young plants set out in it. Behind it
the creek bubbled merrily and a neat stone path led from
the garden to the kitchen door. Pansies and sweet
alyssum bloomed along the walk and there were
hollyhocks against the back wall of the house. The
bricks looked bright and the trim around the windows
and the kitchen door was fresh and white. Chickens and
ducks were squawking and flapping to let her know she
was intruding and a pair of geese scurried across the
grass towards her. Down past the creek a cow and a
small flock of sheep were browsing. Beyond, where
there should have been a field of crab grass and burdock,
was an apple orchard in full bloom.

"This time it's me," whispered Rose. "I've shifted."

SUSAN

"Susan!" A fretful voice called from the house. "Susan, Suusaan!"

"Oh, Lord's mercy, there she is again," sighed the girl. "I don't know where you come from but you best go back there right soon." She paused. "You aren't lost or nothing?"

Rose stared at Susan, not really hearing her.

"Are you lost?" Susan repeated.

"Lost?"

"Susan!" cried the voice.

"Stay here. I'll be back. But mind you don't go helping yourself to nothing."

"Susan!" The tone had become imperious. Off went Susan on the run.

Rose sat down at the edge of the garden. She couldn't believe what had happened. She moved her hand slowly over the soft spring grass. She looked around at the sheep, the neat little garden, the geese, and the chickens who having assured themselves that she was harmless had stopped squawking and were clucking peacefully as they toddled and scrabbled around the yard.

"It's true," she whispered. "I have shifted. And that girl — Susan — *is* the girl I saw making the bed in Aunt

Nan's house — in this house," she amended, realizing that although it looked new and bright, this was the same house she hated so much for being old and ugly. Dazed, she got up and started walking around to the front.

It was certainly the same house, the same back porch, the same shed except that this one was strong and straight and, peering inside, she could see that it was full of things: a wood pile, a big wooden tub with a scrub board stuck in it, old newspapers and an assortment of unidentifiable junk. There was a porch along the front of the house, its roof supported by white posts, carved at the upper corners in elaborate curves and curlicues. Dark green shutters opened out from all the windows.

The tangle of bushes that grew so close to the eastern side of the Henrys' house was gone. Instead there were three large lilac bushes in full bloom. Beyond, partly hidden by the foliage, was a long open-fronted drive-shed where Rose could see an old-fashioned carriage and a wagon parked side by side. Lily of the valley grew in flower beds on either side of the front door. In the middle of the yard was a well with a stone wall around it and a steep roof above it. Out on the road was a row of tall elm trees.

It was a fairytale day. The sun shone warm on the soft red brick of the house and turned the creek and the bay beyond to glittering reflections of its own brilliance. To the west and across the road, apple orchards were a haze of pink and white blossoms. Down past the creek, hawthorn trees covered with tiny white flowers grew singly and in clusters like giant bouquets. Bees hummed in the small chestnut tree in the front yard, and everywhere birds were trilling and calling to each other through the trees.

Nearby someone played a few notes on a flute. Rose looked around. There was no one in sight. The notes sounded again, above her. She looked up and saw a boy with blond hair sitting on the roof of the drive-shed. He was intent on his music and had not seen her. She was trying to decide whether or not to speak when Susan came around the corner of the house.

"There you are," she said, coming towards Rose.

"Damn!" said the boy.

"Oh, Will!"

"Well I almost had him and now he's gone. Susan why did you have to —— Who's that?"

"I dunno. He says he's lost," said Susan.

"What are you playing?" asked Rose. It didn't occur to her to wonder at her boldness in speaking up. Talking to Will and Susan came so easily, without shyness or thought.

"I'm trying to talk to the birds. It's an experiment," answered the boy crossly.

"Mebbe the birds don't want to talk to you," said Susan good naturedly. "Come along down off of there and help this boy find out where he belongs." She turned to Rose, "You can't have come far," she said reassuringly. "Strangers don't much find their way down this road — unless mebbe you came off of a schooner what docked over the other side of the bay. Did you?"

"I don't. . . ." Rose hesitated, not sure what to say. "I come from New York City. Yes, from New York and I'm not a boy, I'm Rose."

"I thought you was pretty for a boy," said Susan, "only your hair is awful short and girls don't wear britches around here." She looked at Rose's jeans. Although she said nothing more, surprise showed clearly in the way her eyes widened. "Well, I'm Susan and this here's Will."

"How do you do?" Rose put out her hand and Susan took it shyly.

"New York City's quite a piece away, ain't it? It must be awful hard with the war on and all that."

"Oh," said Rose vaguely, wondering what Susan could mean. "It's awfully big and noisy in New York. I think this place is better."

"Is it?" Will peered down at her from the roof as though she were some exotic bird that had just dropped into the yard. "City folks don't generally care much for the country."

"See here," Susan asked anxiously, "is your schooner like to go off without you? Hadn't we better help find her?"

"Schooner?"

"Your schooner, the ship you come over on."

"Oh, my schooner, uh — no, it's all right. It's going to be here for ages."

"Ain't that grand," said Susan. "I got my half-day tomorrow and me and Will can show you around if you like. I'm hired girl here and I got to get back to work now but Will, he belongs here so he can help you find where your ship's docked. Does your pa own it? Has all the boys gone to war? Is that why you're dressed like a boy? Around here nobody'll take a girl on the boats — except to work as cook. Only you got to be a good bit older."

''Yes, my father owns the ship, so it's all right for me to stay here tonight.'' The words tumbled out of her in her anxiety not to appear too outlandish.

''You can't stay here,'' said Susan. ''I don't think so,'' said Will, both at the same time.

''You see,'' Susan apologized, ''Will's ma she ain't so good. Will's pa fell off of a roof in a barn raising and died a couple of years back and that same year Will's brother Adam he died of the chills and his ma ain't been the same since. She don't open her house much to strangers. I guess I'm the most stranger that's been near the place since Adam died except for the hired man who used to come and do the heavy chores. There ain't much farming here now. We only got them few sheep and geese and chickens and one cow. Bothers works the farm. Will helps and he's going to take it on when he's finished growing but ——''

''Susan! Susan!''

''There's the missus. Will, you gotta show Rose how to get back to her schooner. Will you come back tomorrow?'' she asked eagerly. Rose promised and Susan smiled, and when Susan smiled it was as though the whole world grew brighter. She ran off as Will slid down from the roof and dropped to the ground. Rose could see now that he was a year or so older than her and almost a foot taller, a serious-looking boy with a thin face and blue eyes. He was wearing a heavy grey shirt and brown woolen britches. His leather boots were laced to the knees. He stuffed his flute into a pocket, and started towards the road.

''Come along,'' he said curtly. He stopped and turned. ''Nope, be shorter by the boat.'' He strode off towards the bay, and not sure what else to do, Rose followed him across the backyard, over the two wide planks that bridged the creek and down to the bay where a small rowboat was tied to a dock. Will leaned over to untie it.

"You get in first," he said.

Rose had been thinking furiously. "Will, did you ever want to run away?" She did not look directly at him.

"Is that what you done?"

"I want to stay here," Rose answered. "I could stay over there." She pointed towards the big red barn just west of the orchard, the roof and back of which could be seen from the dock.

Will looked uncomfortable. "There ain't nothing here for a strange girl to do, and you're awful little." He flushed. "And dainty even in them britches. If you was a boy mebbe I might sneak you out something to eat and give you a hand finding work and a place to stay. Around here nobody gives farm work — or smithing or milling or nothing — to a girl, and without they know you who's going to take you on for a hired girl?"

Rose hadn't thought about the complication of work. She had simply said the first thing that had come to mind. Now she realized she needed time to think. "I guess I'd better go back then," she said quickly. "But I'm coming again tomorrow."

Will nodded. "You want me to take you across the bay?" He looked puzzled and uneasy.

"No, it's all right. I'd rather walk. I came down the road. I only said I was lost because I wanted to stay here. I'll see you tomorrow."

Will nodded again. She could feel his eyes following her as she walked back up past the house and started down the road. When she was sure he could no longer see her she sat down on a rock beside the road to decide what to do next.

She was not going back to Aunt Nan's and Uncle Bob's. She realized they would never know where she had gone, nor she figured would they care. That thought brought a swift, unexpected twinge of pain. She put the Henrys from her thoughts, rested her elbows on her knees and put her chin in her hands. She looked down at her new running shoes and wriggled her toes inside them. She felt scared but excited by what had happened. She couldn't sit still. She jumped up and walked along the road, stopping by a wooden bridge that went over the creek.

"I'm really not going back," she said out loud, startling a blackbird out of a nearby bush. "I don't have to. I could stay here always. I can talk to these people ——" she stopped, realizing with a surge of elation that it was true. Talking to Will and Susan was easy, as easy as talking to people in her daydreams. She was shaken by a thought, "Maybe *this* is where I'm supposed to be. Maybe I belong here." She gazed around at the countryside in wonder. It all seemed brighter and more interesting than any place she had ever seen. Each blade of grass, each tree branch seemed magical. She walked on, savouring every detail, hugging herself with delight.

The road was different from the one that ran past the Henrys' house. It was more like two dirt tracks with grass and weeds and wild flowers growing between and, on either side, the rail fences, the tall trees and dense bushes. It was like walking through a wood except that the bright sunlight through the leaves revealed the fences and fields and pastures beyond. She came to an opening in the brush, climbed over the fence and sat down under a small tree at the edge of the pasture.

"I wonder what Aunt Nan would think if she knew, I wonder if Mrs. Morrissay knew all the time that I was coming here. I wonder if she came to get me. I wonder if I'll see her here. I wonder. . . ." Rose fell fast asleep.

When she woke up it was night and she was stiff and cold and hungry. There was neither moon nor stars. The blackness was smothering. She got up. Shoving her hands into her pockets and standing tall to make herself feel bigger and braver, she scrambled over the fence and started back towards the house. Young frogs were crik-criking in a nearby swamp. There was a wind in the trees, rustling the leaves and rattling in the underbrush. In the distance an owl hooted his never-ending hollow hoot and, close by, a whippoorwill whistled softly.

A dog barked across the bay. "The country is full of terrible noises," whispered Rose. "I wish they had street lights." Her pace quickened until she was almost running. As her eyes grew accustomed to the dark she could pick out bushes and spaces, and at last the bushes ended, there was a row of trees, a lawn and a big square house. A dog growled and began to bark. A chain rattled. A light flickered in one of the windows and went out. Rose kept to the far side of the road, her teeth chattering with cold and fear.

"This isn't Will and Susan's house," she whispered. "I must have walked the wrong way. I may have gone down all sorts of wrong roads by now. I don't know where I am."

She was terrified of the dog but she was so afraid of

going farther in the wrong direction and losing herself completely that she decided to stay where she was. She tried to reassure herself by telling herself the dog must be securely tied up.

She sat down across the road from the house, hugging herself against the cold, dozing now and then, springing to her feet every time the dog whined or growled. She thought a lot about Will and Susan. She wondered how old they were, what year it might be, what war was going on in New York. There was nothing in this tranquil countryside or the way Will and Susan spoke or dressed to give her a clue.

At last a bird called, one bird with one long monotonous whistle. The sky lightened. Rose could see the farmhouse, shed and barn across the road. She stood up and studied the road in each direction.

"I suppose I'll have to try them both," she said aloud. The dog growled. She could see now that he was a large, unkempt-looking hound. "I'm glad you are chained up," called Rose softly as she hurried off. She was cold and hungry but filled with a buoyancy she had never known before. She was wet with dew, and the grass was wet, but the morning breeze felt friendly, the sky glowed with a delicate pink. The lowing of the cows, the barking of dogs and the regular crowing of roosters were like a morning chorus. Rose sang in accompaniment as she tramped along past houses and barns and over a low stone bridge.

She stopped at last by an open field, trying to get her bearings. She leaned on the top rail of a cedar fence and looked across the bay. She blinked twice. She was looking at the back of Will and Susan's house, the Henrys' house, her house. There was the garden, the cow tethered near the water and, suddenly, there was the sound of Will's flute, sharp and clear across the water.

With a sigh of relief, Rose clambered over the fence and ran across the field to the edge of the bay. From there she could see Will sitting in the rowboat just off his own shore.

"Will!" she called.

Will looked around, shook his fist and threw the flute down in exasperation.

"Will! It's me. I'm over here. Can you come and get me?"

"I've half a mind not to," he shouted, but he picked up the oars and started rowing towards her. She watched impatiently as the boat came closer. It probably did not take more than five minutes but it seemed like half an hour.

Before the boat even touched her shore, Will said crossly, "That's the second time you spoiled it. Why'd you have to call right then?"

"I wanted you to see me."

"Well, I see you."

"I'm hungry."

"Oh, get in. I got some bread and cheese you can have." He reached into a sack he had stowed under the bow seat and pulled out cheese, bread, and four slices of dried apple. Rose perched on the seat opposite him and ate greedily.

"You didn't go back to your schooner," he said.

"No."

"Where'd you stay?"

"In a field and on the road."

"Wasn't you cold?"

"Yes, a little," she mumbled through a mouth full of cheese and apple.

Will offered her a jacket that was stuffed under his seat, and gratefully she accepted. He stared at her curiously for a moment but he asked nothing more about where she had been or why. "I wasn't planning to go home for a while yet but I'll take you to the shore. Susan's free after dinner if you want to wait around."

Rose did not want to spend the day in Will's backyard, or walking up and down the road. "I'll stay here with you," she said. "I know how to be quiet." She remembered, as she said it, the hours spent sitting at dinner while her grandmother talked business or discussed politics with friends. She made herself comfortable in the bottom of the boat, her back against the stern seat. Will frowned at her but clearly he had decided, for whatever reason, not to argue with her.

"O.K.," he said, "but you got to be awful still." With one oar he pushed the boat off the shallows and began to row across the bay. Rose had only been in boats in Central Park in New York, and in Venice, places where a man got paid to take people out for an hour. Those times had never seemed real the way this did.

Will rowed steadily across the bay and past his own house. He anchored close to the shore by a little wood. He sat back, listening. Rose listened too, and looked. The woods were full of sunlight and shade. The white and wine-red flowers that Will said were trilliums, the violets, and the speckled adders tongues, covered the ground in bright patterns. The smell of spring was sweet and sharp. The redwing blackbirds mixed their metallic

complaints with the pretty songs of the orioles and the
bluebirds. She watched the tiny water bugs skating
across the surface of the bay and the gauzy red and blue
and green dragonflies like miniature dancers lighting
here and there on the pond lilies and cattails, and on the
golden marsh marigolds growing thickly along the
shore. Down through the water, minnows darted in and
out among the weeds, and grey and brown stones
gleamed in the dappled sunlight. She stared at her reflec-
tion in the still, clear water and it stared solemnly back
at her. For the first time she did not dislike it. She
thought how much a part of the woods Will looked, his
hair sun-golden, his face and hands as brown as the
dried leaves, his eyes deep blue as the violets.

He had picked up his flute and he played a few notes.
Rose listened. She forgot where she was. She forgot who
she was. She knew only the sounds of the birds and the
flute. She became part of the woods and the water, of
the boat and Will.

The flute played a melody. Overhead a bird sang four
notes. Pip-pip-pip-pip. The flute paused, then responded
in the same four notes. The bird pipped again. The flute
replied. The bird sang, ce-o-lay, ce-o-lay. Very softly the
flute sang back, a conversation. Finally the bird trilled a
long series of rich high notes, paused, gave a little final
pip-pip-pip-pip and, with a flutter of his wings, flew off.

Gradually Rose came back to herself, back to the boat
and to Will sitting on the seat opposite grinning at her.
He put down his flute. "You got good luck in you," he
said quietly. "I been trying to do that for months."

Rose felt a smile grow inside her, almost in spite of
herself. She felt very happy. The thought came, sud-

denly and unbidden, that she loved Will. "I'm going to marry Will," she decided. Sure he must have read her mind, she blushed. She had never before even thought about loving anyone. She felt very self-conscious, and very much aware of Will smiling across at her. She looked down at her feet, at Will's feet, at the oars resting in their locks. Desperate to say something to ease the moment she stammered, "Can . . . can I row?"

"Do you know how?"

"No."

So Will showed her how to hold the oars properly and to pull them at just the right angle and, before long, though a bit lopsidedly and now and again in complete circles, Rose was rowing. She rowed strongly for quite a while, aware all the time of her new, confused feelings. She wanted to reach over to Will as he sat playing softly on his flute. She wanted to tell him she'd decided she meant to marry him. At the same time she was terrified he would find out. Being much practised at willing her mind from things she did not want to think about, she began to ask questions about those things she figured she ought to know.

"What year is this, Will?"

"Huh?"

"What date is it?"

"Why, it's the tenth of June."

"But what year is it?"

"Year? 1862, same as it was yesterday. It's the month of the Methodist camp meeting in Soames though I don't suppose you know about that."

1862. Then it was the Civil War they were talking about. Rose remembered lessons with her grandmother.

The American Civil War, the war between the North and the South, Abraham Lincoln's war. "Is the war on here?" she asked.

"No, it ain't. The war's got nothing to do with us though there's strong feelings about it. We don't mostly hold with the South. We don't believe in slavery. There's a few fellers gone over to join the Union army for the North. Jim Heaton's gone. Mostly we ain't much for war around here but some of us has come over from the States. My ma come from Oswego so all her relatives is there. So did Jim Heaton's."

"I'm glad the war isn't here. I don't even like war movies."

"What's that?"

Rose realized what she had said and quickly changed the subject. "Do you go to school, Will?"

"No more I don't. I went up through the third book but I ain't been in a couple of years. Teacher was a mean feller. He used the switch something terrible even on the little mites. One day he strung Ned Bother up by the thumbs and I punched him. Laid him out flat. I ain't been back since."

"A teacher could do that?"

"Yep. Don't you go to school?"

"My grandmother taught me at home but she died. I guess I was lucky."

"I *guess* so! A body don't learn much crammed in with all them other kids some of 'em only five, some of 'em as old as fifteen, with some devil standing up front for a teacher."

"Can you read?"

"Yep."

"And you can play music, too!"

"Old Mr. Lestrie down to Soames taught me that."
Rose noticed there was awe in Will's voice when he
spoke of the music teacher. "Now give over them oars
and I'll bring us in. I got work to do."

Will rowed them swiftly to the shore, leaped out and
tied up the boat. Rose jumped out after him.

"I'll see you after dinner," he promised, and off he
went whistling up the slope.

Rose stayed a long while by the water thinking about
Will now she was alone. She made a daydream in which
the two of them were living in the big house — "and
Susan can live with us," she decided. She watched Will
as he made his way through the orchard with a bucket
in his hand. "How odd," she thought, "here I am with
Will, and down in the United States the Civil War is
happening."

"The American Civil War was one of the worst wars
in the history of the world." She could still hear her
grandmother's rich voice in her head. "Your great-great-
grandfather and his brothers fought on opposing sides in
that war. He was a Union man — they were for the Confederacy, for the South. When it was over his brothers
were dead and he came to live in the north. He was
never happy but he believed in the union, in one country, and he hated slavery so he had to fight. I remember
him talking about it when he was an old man and I was
a small child. He loved Abraham Lincoln with a passion." Rose had never forgotten those words, partly
because it was such a sad story and partly because of the
unwonted passion in her grandmother's own voice as
she had told it. She had shown Rose a picture of a fierce-

looking old man holding a top hat, and they had taken a trip to Richmond, Virginia, where great-great-grand-father had come from, and to Washington D.C. to see the statue of Abraham Lincoln.

It seemed only a few minutes later when she glanced up to see Will going into the house.

"It can't be dinner time already. It's not dark." She hurried up the slope and stationed herself beside a big maple tree not far from the root cellar. In a few moments Will came out, and Susan was with him. Will was carrying a large basket. Susan smiled and waved. "Here you are," she called, "and we've brought our din-ner to have with you. Come along and let's take it out to the orchard."

They spread a fresh white cloth out under the flower-ing apple trees. On it they put a plate of cold pork and potatoes, dishes of pickles and relish, thick slices of brown bread, a bowl of stewed rhubarb, a pitcher of cream and a cake. Rose thought she had never eaten such a delicious meal in all her life.

When they had eaten everything, Rose and Susan sat with their backs against the trees and Will stretched out on the ground watching a line of ants carry away the last crumbs of cake. Susan had to hear about the night Rose had spent by the road.

"You must have been up as far as Bother's and that dog of theirs is a bad one. Him and me don't get along all that good though he's never offered to bite me yet. You're a brave one. I guess that's why you work on the boats and wear britches," she said admiringly.

Rose looked from Will to Susan. "What I told you isn't true," she said. "I've never been on a ship. I don't have a father. I don't have a mother either."

"Same as me," murmured Susan.

"I don't know if you'll believe me but I'm going to tell you anyway. I came to live with my aunt and uncle in this house one week ago — only, of course, it isn't this house. I mean it *is* this house only it's more than a hundred years from now. I don't know how it happens. It started with Mrs. Morrissay, so I think she has something to do with it." Rose told them the story of her meeting with Mrs. Morrissay, of Aunt Nan, Uncle Bob and the boys. She told them how she had found the root cellar.

Both Will and Susan listened, fascinated. When Rose had finished Susan shook her head slowly. "It don't matter where you come from, Rose. We ain't going to give you away to folks that use you bad." Rose could see that Susan did not believe a word she had said but she did not mind. No one had ever listened to her with such interest.

"That's a fine tale!" Will sat up. "You've even put us Morrissays in it. It's like some of them stories Susan's gran used to tell about ghosts and strange critters back where she come from in Scotland. It's the kind of story you could almost make a song out of." He pulled his flute out of his pocket and played a few notes. "It's kind of sad too, but I guess it's like Susan says, it don't matter where you come from. I guess what matters is where you belong. Me, I ain't always sure. I was born here but Ma comes from across the lake in the States. Now they got this war I feel like it's got something to do with me. My cousin Steve over in Oswego says I'm as much Yankee as him."

"That Steve!" Susan snorted. "He comes here from across the lake with his ma sometimes and every time he comes him and Will get into some kind of trouble. The last time he come — just last summer — he got a hold of Will's pa's old shot-gun and he scared all of Bother's cows out of their pasture and up the road. There wasn't a one of 'em had good milk for a week. Grandpa Bother said he'd be happy to take the gun to Steve any time Will's ma would care to have him.''

Will grinned. "He makes things jump, all right.'' They told other stories about the neighbourhood, tales of storms on the lake that sank whole ships in five minutes, tales of religious camp meetings, of boisterous practical jokes and fights that went on for days. Rose could hardly imagine some of the scenes they described. She realized that Will's name was Morrissay. She learned that Susan's parents had been killed when their sleigh upturned through the ice on the bay and that Will did not want to farm even though he loved the land. Susan talked about being an orphan too, and coming to work for Will's mother. "I'm twelve now. Been here three years.'' Rose could hardly believe Susan was the same age that she was. "I got to do a woman's work,'' said Susan.

It didn't seem like more than a few moments before the sun was low over the bay, and the trees were making long shadows against the ground. Cows were lowing in the distance and, before long, the Morrissays' had joined the mournful chorus. Reluctantly Susan got up. "There goes Pearly,'' she sighed, "and my half-day's done with.''

"What are we going to do about you, Rose?'' asked Will. "Where is she going to stay? I guess mebbe she could stay in the barn for one night.''

Susan agreed. "We'll just have to figure out something else after tomorrow. But first thing in the morning you'll have to be getting back to where you come from — or finding a place that'll take you on as a hired girl. I'm coming, Pearly!" — as the cow bellowed to be milked, and off went Susan, skirts flying, to bring her in.

Will did not get up at once. Now and then he glanced over at Rose. "Them things you said is awful funny," he said finally. "No mind. I guess I might as well show you the barn."

"Don't we have to pick up the things?"

"Yep."

They gathered up the cloth and the empty plates and bowls and carried them to the house. At the kitchen door Will took her share from Rose. "I best go in alone," he said.

From inside his mother called plaintively, "Is that you, Will?"

Through the screen door Rose could see a woman approaching. She was tall with a long, gaunt face, large sunken eyes and grey-blond hair in a tight bun at the back of her head. Suddenly Rose was frightened. It was the look of the woman, so drab, so obviously wretched in a world that was so beautiful. She leaped back. Without thinking where she was going she ran to the root cellar, pulled open the doors and scurried down the steps.

Seconds later, feeling foolish, she went back up the steps — and out into the cold autumn evening of the Henrys' backyard.

WILL

Rose was heartsick. It was like being back in prison, finding herself in the Henrys' cold autumn backyard. Frantically she ran back into the root cellar and out again, once, twice, a dozen times. It was always the same. In a rage of disappointment she made her way through the bushes and into the house where Jimmy (or Brian) said, "Our mother's been looking all over for you. Where did you go?"

"Shut up!" said Rose. She had never said that to anyone. She said it again: "shut up." She gave the cat a shove with her foot and stamped upstairs.

"It's time for dinner," Brian (or Jimmy) called after her in hurt tones, and she realized with a start that it was the same evening it had been when she had found the root cellar and gone into Will and Susan's world. She could hardly bear it. She sat down to dinner in silence and a confusion of bitter thoughts.

Monday she started school. The school bus came at quarter to eight and stopped along the road to pick up noisy, curious children who kept turning to stare at her where she sat in the last seat. The school smelled of

chalk and old running shoes. She was sure the teacher's
"We're glad to have you with us, Rose. I hope you'll be
happy here," was insincere. She did not want anything
to do with the children in her class, and she hated the
playground where everyone pushed and shoved and
chased each other. Several girls came and spoke to her.
She drew her head down into the high neck of her
sweater like a turtle and answered "yes", "no", or "I
don't know" to all their questions. She was afraid of
them, even Alice, the gentle albino girl with the thick
glasses.

A couple of weeks went by. At school, Alice and
Margery, who sat next to Rose, and Margery's friend
Gail all tried making friends but Rose did not want their
friendship, and they left her alone. At home, Aunt Nan
in her casual, chattering fashion, Uncle Bob and George
in their own ways, began to take her for granted. Even
Sam, although he was not gracious about it, seemed to
have accepted her. He once tried to share part of a
chocolate bar with her on the bus. But Rose would have
nothing to do with Sam. The memory of his cruel words
was too sharp. She made no effort to be especially
friendly with any of them, although she did give in to
the twins pleading to tell them a story. She told them
about a princess who could not get back to her own
country, and she made it so sad that they cried.

Even Uncle Bob, who was not very good at noticing
people, said to Aunt Nan one evening in Rose's hearing,
"Do you suppose we insulted that child in some way?"
Aunt Nan said she didn't think so, that they would just
have to be patient because Rose was probably missing
her grandmother.

But it was not her grandmother; it was Will and Susan and a whole lost world.

"I spent just one day there," she lamented, over and over. "One day and now I can't go back!"

Every day after school, while the boys wrangled in the kitchen, she went out to the glade and down the rotted steps into the root cellar. It was always the same. The first time was a shock. Instead of the sturdy inside door that had been there the first time, there was a door as rotten and full of holes as the outside ones and it was hanging by a badly rusted hinge. Inside there were no shelves, no crockery jars. There were only cobwebs and dust and, in one corner, a dead rat. Rose jumped back in horror and fled up the steps, dropping the doors behind her with so much noise she was sure she must have been heard from the house. After that she was quiet, even secretive, and in spite of the dead rat, she still went every day, hoping, praying for whatever magic had been at work that first day. The puzzle of it occupied all her thoughts. She searched her memory for every detail of that day, every move she had made and could find no clue.

She walked up and down the road all the way around the end of the bay. There were tall reeds there where the water had been high in 1862. Nothing looked as it had looked on the night she had walked away from the Morrissays'. The modern road was dirt but it was wide enough for cars to pass each other and on either side there were just fields, no high bushes and trees.

October became November. Some days the creek had ice along its edges and the little hawthorn tree was almost bent double by the wind. Winter came in, bleak and grey, to the island. The low, rolling countryside looked bare and vulnerable. Rose had never been so unhappy in her life.

One afternoon, as she sat at the back of the school bus, she felt as if she could not stand another moment of screaming, fighting kids, and when Jim and Phil Heaton from down the road got off the bus, she got off too. The twins called anxiously after her, ''Rose, Rose, where are you going?'' The Heaton boys looked at her curiously but she paid no attention to any of them. She stuffed her hands into the pockets of her jacket, kicked angrily at a stone that lay in her path, and started walking. It was very cold, but the day was bright. A few white clouds were whipping across the sky like sailboats in a race. Leaves were swirling up from the ground.

''You want to come along over here and give a hand, youngster?'' Rose started. She had been so engrossed in her own thoughts that she hadn't noticed she had stopped by a house. It had an iron fence around it and an old man was standing by the gate with a length of stout wire in his hand.

''Here,'' he said again. He was thin and stooped, with a small tuft of white hair on top of his long face. His eyes were blue — like Will's eyes, Rose thought — and they had smile wrinkles at the corners. His face was kind and his manner easy. Rose went over to him.

''You just hold up the gate so as I can tie it up with this here wire,'' he said. She held while the old man wound the length of wire around the gate and post so that the gate hung evenly and level with the fence. Only then did she look at her surroundings. The big old house, covered with grey stucco, looked somehow familiar, its yard full of trees and surrounded by the iron fence.

"You like my house?" The old man smiled. "How about coming in and having a cup of tea with me?"

Rose went with him. Inside, the big, comfortable kitchen was pleasant and warm. The late afternoon sunlight streamed in through a long window at the back and settled on an old couch along one wall. The floor was covered with a worn linoleum and the walls were hung with calendars and yellowed newspaper clippings. A kettle was steaming on a big, black wood stove.

"Sit you down," said the old man, "sit you down. My name's Tom Bother, but you call me Old Tom, everyone does. That's to tell me from Young Tom though he moved over to Soup Harbour twenty years ago. Nobody here but me any more. You must be the young lady who's come to live up to Henrys' place. I ain't been up there for two, three weeks but I knowed you was coming. I do a bit of work for Mr. Henry now and then."

"How do you do? I'm Rose Larkin."

"That's a nice name," said Old Tom. As he talked he was making tea and putting out buttered corn meal muffins.

"Have one," he offered. "I won prizes with my muffins though it grates on some of the women round here to know it."

Rose perched on the edge of the couch, and listened to Old Tom. He said he was eighty-one years old and had always lived in the same house. "In fact," he said, "Bothers has lived here since 1802 when we built the first cabin in the woods. We come up from the States after we was kicked out, when we wouldn't fight the king in the American Revolution in 1776. We come up along with the Collivers, the Heatons, 'n Morrissays, 'n Yardleys, 'n Andersons. Collivers built the mill and so that's how Collivers' Corners got named after 'em. Yardley's had the smithy and Andersons, Morrissays and Heatons and us was just farmers, clearing the woods and trying to make do and we been here ever since and never budged — hardly a one of us. My grandfather used to tell me about it. He got it from his grandfather who was a little feller when they all come.''

Rose heard him talking on but she wasn't really listening. Morrissays. Old Tom knew Morrissays. And he knew Heatons and Yardleys. Will had talked about Heatons and Yardleys.

''Do you know Heatons and Yardleys and . . . and Morrissays?'' she asked eagerly.

Old Tom laughed. ''Well I *guess* so, they're my neighbours,'' he said. ''Well most of 'em is. There ain't Morrissays around nowadays. The last one died a few years back. The old lady lived — Morrissays always lived — in that house you live in.''

Rose almost said, ''I know,'' but she didn't. She didn't want him to think she was crazy. It made her feel strange hearing him say that Mrs. Morrissay had died. Her Mrs. Morrissay was so very much alive. She ate her corn muffin in silence, wanting to ask more, not sure how to phrase her questions so that they made sense.

''Well,''she said, brushing the crumbs from her lap neatly into her hand, ''I have to go now.''

''Thank you for your help, young lady,'' said Old Tom. He put his hand briefly on her head. ''Come visit with me again. I take kindly to visitors.''

She promised she would. Outside she turned to close the gate carefully after her, and her mouth fell open in surprise — because she recognized the house she had sat across the road from all night after she had left Will and Susan. "Bother's house," Susan had said. Of course. But it was different. It wasn't just the new grey stucco — the shadows were different. The shadows during that long frightening night had seemed as permanent as the house. It came as a surprise to see their long slanting shapes in the late afternoon sun.

She had a sudden electrifying idea. She began to run. She no longer noticed the cold. She was hot with excitement. She ran until she reached the root cellar. Breathlessly she flopped down on the crackling leaves and studied the closed doors. The shadow of the hawthorn tree fell across them parallel to the opening between them.

"Where was it the day I went to Will and Susan's," whispered Rose, "where was it?" She closed her eyes, trying to remember. In her mind she saw the doors revealed by her feet scuffing the leaves away, the trees and bushes making patterns and shadows over them. "Yes," she murmured, "yes it was! It was in the middle. Exactly in the middle." She opened her eyes. The hawthorn's shadow was to the left of the opening, not more than an inch. She waited, her fists clenched anxiously. Had it just been or was it coming? She did not move, her eyes were riveted to the opening.

Slowly, almost imperceptibly, the shadow moved towards the crack. Rose held her breath, her body tense as a runner's waiting for the starting flag. Then, when the shadow fell just where the hook-and-eye latches met, she pulled open the doors, ran down into the root cellar and came up beside the little garden in the Morrissays' backyard.

She sat down beside the creek, letting out long breaths of relief. The chickens were pecking in the garden, the sheep and Pearly the cow were grazing beyond the creek. Only the sound of Pearly's bell tinkling as she moved and the chirping of robins in the trees broke the stillness of the warm afternoon. She hurried down past the creek to the bay, then back up to the orchard looking for Will or Susan. She realized as she approached that the apple trees were not in bloom as they had been last time. They weren't even in leaf.

"Time must be strange here, or at least not the same as ours," she decided.

As she walked through the budding trees in the orchard she felt again the magic of that other day. A squirrel scurried out onto a branch at the sound of her approach and she felt the peacefulness of it all settle over her once again. She heard voices coming towards her. One of them was a deep male voice. In a sudden panic lest she be discovered by strangers, she hid behind the nearest tree. Within seconds the voices were almost beside her. Then whoever it was stopped.

"And don't you dare breathe a single word of what I told you to Ma or I'll cast a spell on you, Susan Anderson. There's ways and ways of casting spells and you know it because it was your own gran who told us, and some of 'em you can do from far away and I'll do 'em for certain sure if you tell."

Rose peered out from behind her tree. It was Susan and Will, a taller, older Will with a deep cracking voice, like George's. He was over six feet tall now and his straw-white hair had darkened to a deep gold colour. Susan was different, too. She was taller than Rose and looked older. Rose was horrified. How old were they? How much time had gone by?

"She ain't to know," said Will fiercely.

"But Will," Susan clasped and unclasped her hands nervously in front of her. "If you run away it'll kill your ma. It truly will. She says there's a curse on your family."

"I know what Ma says. Don't she say it every morning of my life? I can't hardly stand to be around. It's like living with the dead, living here. Why don't she go home to Oswego? My aunts are jolly folks and so are my cousins. She only come here to marry Pa. Her folks don't belong here and I don't belong here neither. I'm going to take myself back there, and Steve and me we're going to join up. They been asking for recruits again and we're ——"

"Will Morrissay! You're never going to do that!" gasped Susan. Will clapped his hands over Susan's mouth. "Shut up! I never meant to tell that! Now you got to promise silence. Silence! Because I don't want no one hereabouts to know where I gone. And if you don't promise I'm going to break both your arms and throw you in the bay. Do you hear?"

Susan nodded. Will took his hand from her mouth but he held her arms firmly. "Are you promising?"

"Will, I. . . ."

"Both your arms," he said grimly, staring fixedly into her eyes. "Both your arms."

"I promise," said Susan softly, "and not because of

your stupid threats but because if it matters so much to you I'm not going to tell but, oh Will, why do you have to go and join up? It ain't our war. We got no part in it. You heard what happened in Soames the other day. That Yankee got arrested for trying to recruit our boys. Right here to Collivers' Corners. Benny Bother told Joey Heaton he was going to set his dogs on any of them Yankees that come here to fetch our Canadian boys to fight in the rebellion. It ain't our war, Will!"

"It's part mine, Susan, it's part mine. My ma come from the States. Her country needs soldiers bad. The war's been going on for three years and thing's is desperate. Steve told me last time he come here that him and Aunt Min and them all went down to New York City when Abraham Lincoln was there and they seen him. He says Lincoln's all but a saint and I believe him. Lincoln freed the slaves from those rich people in the South — and you know yourself how some of them black peoples come across the lake to get away from being slaves and the terrible things they told about being beaten and put in chains and made to work like animals. Well, after this war there ain't going to be no more slaves and, what's more, them states in the South ain't going to be able to quit the United States just because they happen to feel like it."

"Well I don't care if they do or don't."

"Well I care and Steve says just about all the boys from Oswego County who can walk have gone. One of the regiments was home in February and they was recruiting — and he's going to go if I'll go with him. And I'm going. I'm shipping out with the *Eliza Fisher*. She's heading for Oswego today with a load of grain and Captain Soames says he's got a day's work I can do. When I get there I'm going off with Steve to join up."

"Will!" Susan took hold of his arms. "Who's going to look after things for your ma?"

"Who'd look after 'em if I was dead?"

"I don't know but you ain't dead — not yet, you ain't. Oh, Will!"

"Susan, I got to go. I made up my mind. It's a thing I got to do."

They were both silent, not looking at each other, not really looking away either. Finally Will took his hands from Susan's arms. He shouldered the small pack that he had set beside him on the grass. "Goodbye," he said. "I'd leave you something for a keepsake only I don't know what it'd be."

"I got a bit of paper with a song you made written on it. I'll keep that. Here, you take my locket." Susan reached up and undid the chain around her neck.

"Susan, you can't give that! It was your gran's."

"Take it."

Will stuffed the locket in his pocket. He grabbed Susan's hands. "You remember what you promised," he said and off he went on his long legs, not once looking back.

Susan stood unmoving as the trees. Then, with her head down, hugging herself tightly with both arms she ran from the orchard.

Rose slowly came out from behind the tree, stupefied. She stared at the spot where Will and Susan had stood. How could this happen? How could they grow older like that and leave her behind? How could Will just go off to

the war? She pounded the trunk of the tree furiously
with her fists. She felt cheated, betrayed. Pale and shaking she ran back through the orchard, past the sheep and
the hens, down the steps into the root cellar and back up
into the world she hated so much.

A SONG AND
A SILVER ROSE

The next afternoon Rose went down the root cellar steps
with great trepidation. She was furious with herself for
having run away. "Stupid, stupid," she had told herself
off and on all day. "How can I fix it if I'm not even
there?" For she had determined to set her world to
rights, to find out where Will had gone and get him
back. She did not mean to return to the Henrys again so
she had packed her overnight bag with everything she
felt she might need — her extra pair of jeans, shirts,
socks and underwear, her pajamas and her treasures —
and she had gone to find Susan.

She came up the steps into a bright summer morning.
The sky was pale blue. A breeze was blowing gently
through the leaves of the big maple tree and faintly stirring the roses and wood geraniums beside the cellar
door. Susan was hanging laundry out beyond the vegetable garden. Rose stood uncertainly on the path, her
suitcase in one hand. She felt a bit shy with this bigger,
older Susan, but again, the knowledge that she was
where she belonged made her bold.

She cleared her throat. Susan let out a shriek.

"It's me — Rose. Did I scare you?"

Susan's eyes grew big and round. Her mouth gaped open. She clutched at the clothesline for support.

"It's just me," said Rose again.

"It *is* Rose," Susan whispered, "It is. . . . Lord's mercy!"

"I came back."

"I see that, but wherever did you come from? Oh, my, you did give me a start!" Susan shook her head. She began again to hang out the laundry, all the while looking nervously at Rose.

Rose was relieved to see that Susan didn't look any older than she had the day before. All the same she asked, to make sure, "Where's Will?"

Susan had finished her work but she had not moved. She still watched Rose warily.

"Will's gone off, Rose."

"I know that."

"You know?"

"I was hiding behind a tree and I heard."

"You was hiding behind a tree?"

"I came back to find you and when I heard talking in the orchard, and it didn't sound like you, I was scared so I hid. When was it Susan? How long ago I mean."

"You ought to know that if you was here."

"I was here. Listen." And Rose recited to Susan a good deal of the conversation she had overheard in the orchard. To her dismay it brought tears to Susan's eyes.

"It's just we ain't heard from Will in eight months," said Susan.

"Eight months!" Rose was aghast. "How long ago did he go?"

"It was a year in April."

"A year! Has he sent letters?"

"At first he sent 'em. He never told much but they was letters all the same and they told he was all right. I got 'em all saved. But there ain't been none since January, and the war's been over for four months now."

"The war's over?" Rose searched her memory for the date of the end of the war. "What year is it now, Susan?"

"It's the 16th of August in 1865, and the war's been done since April and poor Mr. Lincoln shot dead in the theatre and cold in his grave by now, and they still haven't caught that crazy Mr. Booth who done it. If you come from New York like you said, how come you don't know that? How come you. . . ." Susan stopped. She studied Rose intently. "There's something queer about you," she said, then added quickly, "I don't mean nothing by that, I don't think you're looney or nothing, it's just there's things I can't figure out about you. You come here three years back. You said you was running away and you wanted to stay here so bad. Then, quick's a flick of a cow's tail, you was gone. Will went in the house for no more than three minutes and when he come out you was gone and we ain't set eyes on you from that moment to this. And here you are as though it was yesterday you come and you ain't changed. Not growed, nor changed. Not a hair of you. You even got the same clothes on. It gives me the jitters."

"I know," said Rose remembering the day Mrs. Morrissay came through her bedroom wall. "I don't understand it either but I did tell you, Susan, I did. I told you and Will when we were having our picnic over in the apple trees but you didn't believe me. I do come from New

York, only I come from New York more than a hundred years from now. You have to believe me because it's true. It's three years ago for you but for me it's only three weeks. I haven't grown any because I'm only three weeks older.

"I didn't mean to disappear that day. I ran down into the cellar because I was scared and then I got stuck and it took me all this time to figure out how to get back. It was because of the shadow —— don't, Susan, don't!" she begged, because Susan was backing away, her eyes wide with fright. "I'm real. Really I'm real. Stop looking at me like that! It's just this thing with the root cellar!"

"What thing?" asked Susan, keeping a good distance between herself and Rose.

Rose set her bag down. She looked at the open doors of the root cellar, and said slowly, "Well, it's . . . it's . . . I think it's because of Mrs. Morrissay. I don't mean Will's mother, it's another Mrs. Morrissay. She started it but I'm not sure she knew she was doing it. Anyway she showed up the day I came to live in this house and she stayed until I found the root cellar. I told you about that. Then, after we had our picnic, Will's mother scared me and I ran back down into the cellar. When I went back up the stairs I was in Aunt Nan's time. I tried and tried to come back but I only found out today how to do it. There's a little hawthorn tree — it's like that one over on the other side of the creek — and when the shadow from that tree falls exactly between the two doors that lead to the root cellar, I can open the doors, go into the cellar and come up in your time. Do you understand now?"

"How old are you, Rose?"

"I'm twelve."

"You said you was twelve when you came here before."

"I was. I keep telling you, Susan, it was only three weeks ago for me. I wish it wasn't because now you're three years older and Will isn't here!" She looked accusingly at Susan. In her frustration she felt that it was somehow Susan's fault. "Anyway," she said impatiently, "what we have to do now is find Will."

Susan sat down on the ground, put her head in her hands and burst into tears. Rose had never been with anyone crying before. She felt embarrassed and awkward. After a long, fidgety moment she put out her hand and touched the top of Susan's bowed head. Susan jumped back in fright.

"You might be a ghost," she whispered and suddenly it all struck Rose as funny. Mrs. Morrissay, herself, Will, the whole Henry family, maybe they were all ghosts. She began to laugh, loud bellowing laughs such as she had never laughed before in her life. She laughed so hard she had to sit down, shaking with laughter.

"Do I look like a ghost? Or feel like a ghost? Susan, I'm not a ghost."

"You don't and that's a fact," said Susan. She dried her eyes on her apron, and smiled her wide, warm smile. "No, you ain't a day older nor a hair changed from what you was three years ago and if you can get along with the queerness of it then I suppose so can I."

Then Rose told Susan again how she had found the root cellar. Together they marvelled over the strangeness of it, and Rose told her how she felt that this world was where she really belonged. Then she said confidently, "I know Will's alive somewhere. We have to find out where so we can bring him home."

"We can't do that," said Susan, "we wouldn't know where t'start. It was an awful big war and them things can't be as easy to sort out as eggs or apples."

Rose jumped to her feet. "Yes, they can!" She cried. "Yes, they can. They can be if all you have to do is look in history books for them. Back at Aunt Nan's or in the library in Soames or somewhere there must be a lot of books that tell about the Civil War."

"But, Rose, them books, even if you can find 'em, ain't going to say what happened to William Morrissay from the Hawthorn Bay Canada West."

"No, I guess not." Rose felt deflated. Then she brightened. "Maybe old Tom Bother knows. He says his family's always lived here."

"Bothers lives up the road."

"And they do on Aunt Nan's road, at least one does, and I can ask him and maybe there are other people who might know. I'll go and find out. I'll come back tomorrow night." Rose stopped short. "Susan, what if I come tomorrow night and another three years have gone or maybe even more? How can we make it be the same time for you as it is for me?"

"I don't know," said Susan unhappily. "I don't know, unless mebbe if we . . . no, I guess there ain't a sure way to do it."

"What were you going to say?"

"I was going to say there's them believes if you give a promise and a keepsake then you always come back when you say. But Will left me a keepsake and I give him one and he ain't come back."

"Did you say *when* though? I heard you doing that because I was behind the tree and I don't remember that you said when."

"No, that's so, I didn't."

"So we can try it. I could leave you my suitcase."

Susan was doubtful. "That ain't really a keepsake. A keepsake's got to be something you care a good deal about. It's like leaving a bit of yourself for the promise."

"Here." Rose reached up and undid the chain around her neck. "You gave Will your locket. So you have mine. It's a rose for me."

Susan took the silver rose and held it in the palm of her hand. "Ain't it pretty," she said softly.

"It came from someone a long time ago. My father gave it to my mother when they got married and my mother gave it to me when I was born. My grandmother told me. It's what I care most about in all the world so if I leave it with you then it has to mean I'll come back when I say. Here, I'll put it on you."

Carefully Rose clasped the chain around Susan's neck. Susan said, "Wait here," and ran into the house. In less than two minutes she was back. "Here. You take Will's song he left me. It was what he wrote after the day we was all together in the orchard. It's my keepsake from him, and it's what I care most about in all the world. This way you got a keepsake from both of us."

The scrap of paper had been carefully folded and wrapped in a bit of flowered cloth. Rose put it in the deep pocket of her jeans. She started towards the steps. She turned back and solemnly shook Susan's hand. "There, that seals it. When I come back the same amount of time will have passed for both of us. Goodbye." She ran down the steps, this time without looking back.

STOWAWAY

When Rose came into the kitchen Aunt Nan was getting supper and chattering away about the story she was writing. Uncle Bob was sitting on the high stool beside the stove, drinking coffee and listening.

"I want to know about the Civil War," said Rose, not looking directly at either of them. She felt like a cheat. It suddenly didn't seem fair to be accepting their hospitality. She felt as though she ought to tell them where she was going but she couldn't.

"The Civil War?" asked Aunt Nan. "Do you mean the Spanish Civil War or the English Civil War or the American Civil War?"

"The American. Abraham Lincoln's war."

"Are you doing a project, dear? I guess you could start with the encyclopaedias. They're on the bottom shelf of the bookcase in my writing room."

Rose went at once to find the books.

"Funny girl," she heard Aunt Nan say, but this time she did not mind. She pulled volume after volume off the shelf until she found what she was looking for. She sat cross-legged on the floor in front of the bookshelf and read.

"The American Civil War, also called the War Between the States, the War of the Rebellion, and the War for Southern Independence, was a war between the eleven states of the south and the states and territories of the north. The causes of the war were many and complicated but, although emotions ran high on both sides on the issue of slavery, the basic cause was economic. The issue was the right of states to their own government. Abraham Lincoln was elected president in 1860 as an advocate of strong central government. . . . The south could not accept Lincoln. The war began when seven states in the south seceded from the Union and fired on the federal Fort Sumter in Charleston, South Carolina, on 12 April, 1861. Soon afterwards the other five southern states seceded and formed the Confederate States of America under the presidency of Jefferson Davis. Its capital was at Richmond, Virginia. . . . Slavery was outlawed when Lincoln issued his emancipation proclamation in 1862. This further inflamed the south. . . .

"The war ended on 9 April, 1865, when Robert E. Lee, general of the Army of the Confederacy, surrendered to Ulysses S. Grant, general of the U.S. army, at Appomattox, Virginia."

The encyclopaedia went on to say that the war was a bitter one. Robert E. Lee, a descendant of George Washington's wife, had been a graduate of West Point Military Academy and had freed all his slaves, but he had loved his home state of Virginia too much to fight against it. Rose remembered again her grandmother's stories of her great-great-grandfather.

The encyclopaedia had pages of descriptions of battles and pictures of generals from both sides.

"It's interesting," thought Rose, "but Susan is right — it isn't going to say a single word about Will."

That afternoon she got off the bus at Old Tom Bother's. She found him out behind his house, wrapping a piece of tin around a young birch tree.

"Just making sure the rabbits won't get at it in the winter," he told her. "I like the rabbits. I always throw out bread for 'em but I don't like them chewing on my trees. Come along inside." Rose liked Old Tom. He said "mebbe" the way Will and Susan did, and talked in their same easy, twangy way.

Settled comfortably on the kitchen couch, Rose asked him: "Can you tell me things about the people in Collivers' Corners and Soames in the Civil War?"

"The Civil War? The War of the Rebellion in the States you mean?"

"Yes."

"Let me see now. I remember my old dad used to say we sold a lot of wheat in that war. Collivers and Soames and even my old grandpa made good money selling wheat to the Union army. It went by schooner across the lake. There was busy shipping in those days. There was always schooners in and out of here. There was wharves all along the Hawthorn Bay. All the big farms shipped wheat and barley, and anything else they could sell, over to Rochester and Oswego. Boys around here used to earn their money shipping out for a day or a week or sometimes a lifetime. And sometimes they was known to stow away when they couldn't get a berth and then go off and find themselves work in the States. My old dad was a great hand to go off on the schooners. I never did. It wasn't so popular when I was a boy. Wasn't quite the trade no more neither. Barley was finished. Wheat wasn't so big. The railroad come through in '78 and there wasn't much call for shipping. It's all gone now. There's nothing on the lake but yachts and a bit of fishing. But you know this whole island was built on shipping.''

"What about the people around here? Didn't some of them go and fight in the Civil War?''

"Yes, they did. I remember Dad saying there was a Whittier boy from here got killed.''

"Didn't . . . didn't one of the Morrissays go?''

"Mebbe so. I don't know much about that war, except that we sold a lot of wheat. Canada had no part in the war, though of course around here many people had relatives across the lake in New York. What made you think of Morrissays?''

"Well, you said they used to live in our house — I mean in the Henrys' house.''

"Oh did I? Well of course there always was Morrissays in that house right from the start. When I was a boy there was just the old lady but she had a young relative from Winnipeg every summer. Name was George Anderson. He used to come every year and we had grand times together when we was boys. The old lady was good to us. I still remember how particular she was about that house. Loved it. It's a shame what happened to it after she died. Nobody lived there more than two, three years, excepting the racoons. I hope you folks plan to stay. Be good to see it put back in shape.''

Rose said nothing. She wished he wouldn't talk so about ''putting the old house back in shape.'' It made her feel slightly guilty. She got up to leave. She was beginning to feel discouraged about finding out where Will had gone. There was only one place left where she could think to search.

"Where's Oswego?" she asked.

"Why it's just across the lake. About sixty miles as the crow flies."

"How do you get there?"

Old Tom scratched his head. "Well, back when I was a boy, we went by schooner as I told you, but nowadays I expect you have to go all the way around the lake in a car, or mebbe there's a bus. But now I think of it, if you're bent on getting to Oswego I believe your Uncle Bob's going there this weekend."

"This weekend?"

"I believe so."

"Then I'm going with him. Goodbye Old Tom, thanks for the tea and everything." She grabbed her jacket and hurried out the door and up the road.

Uncle Bob had just come in when she got there.

"When are you going to Oswego?" she demanded.

He blinked and drew back in surprise.

"When are you going to Oswego?" she asked again.

"Well, Rose, as a matter of fact I'm going there this weekend. We're leaving tomorrow morning."

"I'm going with you."

"No you're not." George came across the room, slapped the huge pile of toast he was carrying onto the table and wagged his finger at her. "No you're not. Sam's going and I'm going. Mother's not coming and the twins aren't coming and you're not coming."

"Afraid so, Rose," said Uncle Bob. "I promised the boys. I've been invited to a Canadian-American environmental conference that's being held in Oswego on Friday and I've promised to take the big boys. An outing for the three of us. We're leaving early tomorrow morning. You must have heard us talking about it?''

Rose hadn't. She had been so engrossed in the strange events of her own life that she had missed everything going on in the Henry household.

''Please, I won't be any trouble,'' she said. Rose had never pleaded for anything in her life before, but she pleaded now. While George shouted, ''No! You can't, you can't!'' and danced up and down around her, she pleaded earnestly and steadily with Uncle Bob to let her go. She might have won if Aunt Nan had not come bursting out of her writing room looking mussed and cross.

''My Lord, what's all this commotion?'' she cried.

''She says she's going on our trip,'' said George indignantly.

''Is Rose going to Oswego with Daddy and Sam and George?'' The twins had come into the room behind their mother and were edging their way around her. ''Are you, Rose, are you?'' they asked anxiously.

''No,'' said Aunt Nan, ''of course not. Rose, this is Sam and George's trip. One of these days we'll have a trip, though I would have thought you'd had enough travel to last a lifetime. Now will you stop all this racket? Who can work with this noise going on! Rose, why don't you set the table, and I'll be out in a few minutes and start supper.''

Rose set to work without a murmur. She had made up her mind that she was going to Oswego. Even while she was pleading with Uncle Bob to take her she had remembered Old Tom Bother saying, ''sometimes they was known to stow away when they couldn't get a berth,'' and she had decided that she was going to stow away in the station wagon.

The next morning, before the sun was up, her running shoes in her hand, she crept downstairs and out into the front yard.

Dew was heavy on the ground. It was a still morning filled with unexpected November warmth. A flock of geese rose from Heaton's cornfield and, honking and squawking, formed into their V-shaped flight. They passed high over the house, their loud calls and the noisy beating of their wings breaking sharply into the silence. Rose gasped in startled delight and craned her neck to watch. She had a sudden longing to share them with Will. ''I suppose he's seen them lots of times,'' she thought.

A noise from inside the house sent her scuttling behind the big lilac bush.

In a minute or so the twins appeared like two heralds, followed soon after by the rest of the family sleepily lugging raincoats, blankets, suitcases, a huge picnic basket and Uncle Bob's briefcase. They packed it all into the station wagon, unpacked it when Sam pointed out that they had put everything on top of the lunch, and packed it again. ''I wish we could go,'' said the twins wistfully and Rose heard Sam saying, as they trooped back to the house for breakfast, ''I'll put you in my suitcase with my harmonica.''

In an instant Rose had crawled into the back of the station wagon under the raincoats and blankets beside the lunch. It seemed like hours of cramped waiting

before the others came out of the house again, hours
more before they were actually ready to leave — Aunt
Nan had one more last question, one more last warning
about the road. Then she suggested, just as Uncle Bob
put his foot on the gas pedal, that they really shouldn't
leave without saying goodbye to Rose. "Poor kid, she's
probably lonely. Maybe you could have. . . ."

"For heaven's sake, Nan," said Uncle Bob, "why
can't you let sleeping dogs lie," which made George
snort loudly. Uncle Bob put his foot firmly on the ac-
celerator and they were off.

Rose crouched under the blankets and raincoats,
beside the strong smell of chopped egg sandwiches,
while George talked, Sam played his harmonica and Uncle Bob drove silently along winding roads and on and
off ferries. At the border into New York State a gruff-
voiced customs man asked if they had anything in the
car to declare. Uncle Bob assured him they hadn't.

"You want to open up the back?" said the voice.

Rose stopped breathing. She had forgotten about
customs. She had not even remembered to bring her
passport. She heard Uncle Bob's voice as he lifted the
tailgate: "It's our lunch, and our fishing gear in case we
get a chance." He laughed, and told the customs official
about the trip. A hand gave Rose a good punch. She was
sure the blankets were going to be yanked from her. But
they weren't.

"Have a good day then," the voice said cheerfully,
and the tailgate was slammed down. The front door
closed, and they were off. They drove along more winding roads, until the blankets, the raincoats and the smell
of chopped eggs were too much for Rose. She sat up.

"I think I'm going to be sick."

"Good God!" shouted Uncle Bob and the station wagon swerved dangerously.

"I *am* going to be sick," said Rose.

Uncle Bob pulled over to the side of the road. Sam jumped out and threw open the tailgate. Rose crept out of the car and all but fell into the ditch beside the road where she vomited noisily while the others talked angrily among themselves.

"What I'd really like to do," snapped Uncle Bob, when Rose had recovered sufficiently to listen to him, "is leave you right here but there's probably a law against it. What do you suppose would have happened to me, young lady, if the customs and immigration people at the border had found you?"

"We would have said, 'that's our picnic and that's our cousin,' " said Sam.

"And how do you think I would have felt," continued Uncle Bob, ignoring Sam, "and what would you have done?"

"I have my passport at home," said Rose.

"What on earth good would that be? I —— oh, never mind. Get in the back seat. We'll have to find a place where we can call your Aunt Nan. She might be worrying about you though, right now, I can't imagine why."

Rose got into the back seat — as far from the egg sandwiches as she could — and they drove in silence until they came to a village where there was a store with a sign over the door that read *Telephone*.

"You wait here," said Uncle Bob shortly and he and George went inside.

Rose sat very still, feeling ill but triumphant. Sam

played his mouth organ. Uncle Bob and George came
back with bottles of pop.

"Here." Uncle Bob handed her a bottle. "Aunt Nan is
very unhappy about you." No one said anything else to
her for the whole three hours it took to get to Oswego.

At the motel, Uncle Bob asked for an extra room for
Rose.

"I'll pay," said Rose.

"Don't be foolish," Uncle Bob said curtly. Meekly
Rose followed him along the corridor and up the ele-
vator.

Upstairs in her room she could hear the voices of her
cousins through the wall, exploding in wrath against
her. She could not distinguish their words. All she could
hear were angry tones swelling and falling like a stormy
sea.

"I did it!" She smiled jubilantly at herself in the mirror. "I did it and I don't care how angry they are!"

At supper she was content to sit in the silence the
boys maintained towards her. The motel stood beside
the river near the harbour mouth, and through the window she watched a few small fishing boats coming in,
and a sailboat unfurling its sails in the setting sun.

After supper Uncle Bob insisted that they get some
exercise. The boys wouldn't walk with Rose but Uncle
Bob had recovered from his anger and he walked beside
her, and talked about clearing the lake of chemicals and
making the waters of Ontario and New York safe for
wildlife. He said nothing about her being a stowaway.

The river that flowed into the harbour just beyond
their motel appeared to divide the town in half. They
walked up the hill to the east along wide streets lined

with trees and big old houses. It was a pleasant, sleepy-looking town. Rose could not imagine Will going off to war in this quiet place.

"That must be Fort Ontario." Uncle Bob pointed downhill towards the harbour where a few even rooftops showed over a square embankment. "The brochure about the town that came in my conference kit said that it was used as a recruiting centre during the Civil War. That should interest you, Rose — weren't you asking about the Civil War the other night? The fort is still in use, but it's a museum and an archives now too."

The next morning after breakfast Uncle Bob said, "You're on your own now, kids. Anyone who wants to come and listen to the lectures is welcome. George, the one you want is this afternoon." He was so obviously pleased by the way things were going, basking in the pleasure of the company of the people he had already met when he went for his morning paper, that he beamed at the three of them before he left the room.

As soon as he had gone, George turned on Rose. "Don't think you're going to tag after us all day. Boy, I can't see why you had to come. Don't you know when you're not wanted?" He loped out of the dining room, turning once to assure himself that she wasn't following. Sam stood up, hesitated as if he might be going to say something but did not and followed George out of the room.

Rose waited for them both to be out of sight, then she headed for the fort. It was a bright morning and so unseasonably warm that she did not need a coat. Indian summer, Uncle Bob called it. The fort, when she reached it, was like a hollowed-out square on a hill overlooking the harbour. There were two-storey square stone buildings set around it like soldiers on permanent guard. The grounds were neatly clipped and even in November still green. At the entrance a man was selling tickets. Rose paid her money and asked to see the person in charge.

"You can't bother Mr. Ancaster, he's a very busy man." The ticket seller was shocked. Rose stood very straight. "I'm Rose Larkin and I have to see Mr. Ancaster. I'm doing some research for my aunt who's writing a book. She can't travel just now because she's going to have a baby soon." She said it with such assurance that the ticket seller went off, shaking his head, muttering.

In a very few minutes he was back.

"Come on," he said curtly, and led the way into the nearest building, upstairs to a small, dusty office cluttered with old books and documents. A tall, thin, grey-haired man got up from his chair and introduced himself.

"I'm Charles Ancaster, the curator here. What can I do for you?" He was clearly amused.

Rose told him where she came from and that Aunt Nan was writing a true story about a Canadian boy who had joined the army in Oswego during the Civil War. "She needs a list of the boys who went from the island."

"My dear child," said Mr. Ancaster, "there were over twelve thousand men from Oswego County who fought in that war and they were all mustered in the city of Oswego. Some of them were from across the lake, but they didn't all say so. Can you be more specific? Do you know the name of the boy you're looking for? Which recruiting station he might have gone to? Exactly when he joined up? What his regiment was?''

"His name was William Morrissay and he joined in 1864,'' said Rose, catching her breath. It upset her to be talking about Will like this. It made such a stranger of him.

"Well we can get out the lists and have a look,'' Mr. Ancaster looked dubious but he went over to a cupboard and brought out three huge old leather record books and put them on the table that stood by the room's only window. For a long while Rose and Mr. Ancaster scanned the lists of the names of the men and boys who had enlisted to fight in the Union army in 1864. The only sound in the room was the turning of the stiff old pages.

Then they found it. In the beautiful script that lists were written in in the 1860s, the ink brown with age, was the name William Morrissay, age fifteen, fifer, 81st Infantry. Just above it was Stephen Jerue, age fourteen, and the place of residence, for both of them, was given as the city of Oswego. Rose felt sudden sharp tears. There he was. There was Will. And Stephen Jerue must be cousin Steve.

"Isn't that interesting,'' said Mr. Ancaster. "William Morrissay. You say he came from across the lake. Of course a lot of them did and didn't want it known in case their relatives might make a fuss about it. Not all Canadians were sympathetic towards our cause. After all, those people across the lake were refugees from the American Revolution and that was only eighty-five years before the Civil War. I'll just note that name.''

Mr. Ancaster got out a notebook and quickly wrote down the information Rose gave him.

"He was Steve's cousin."

"Stephen Jerue," Mr. Ancaster read, "a drummer and a fifer."

"Will played the flute." Rose suspected the curator would not especially want to know that but she was so eager to share with someone the knowledge that Will had really been there that she had to say it.

"Well, I suppose they would have been glad of a boy who had some knowledge of an instrument, although playing the flute and playing the fife are two very different things you know. I see they both went with the 81st."

"The 81st?"

"The 81st regiment. The regiment was home on leave in January of '64. They'd been through some rough battles. They had first formed up in January of '62, and they'd seen action pretty steadily right from the start — Bottom's Ridge, Seven Pines, Malvern's Hill. They came home for a rest and to gather recruits so I suppose that's when your fellow joined up."

"Oh, no! It was later because there were buds on the trees ——"

Mr. Ancaster chuckled. "You sound as though you'd been there."

Rose nearly said, "I was," but she recovered herself. "We read it in a diary."

"I'd like to see that diary. It might be helpful, fill in some of the blanks in our records."

"Er . . . um. . . ." Rose shifted her weight from one foot to the other. "You see it was Susan's diary really and it doesn't say anything else about the war. Are there any lists that would say when Will came home?"

They looked through three more books of lists and did not find either Steve's or Will's name.

"Does that mean they were killed?" asked Rose in a small voice.

"Not necessarily. The lists are incomplete. In fact, if you or your aunt are researching this boy, I'd appreciate finding out for our records what did happen to him. All this means is that they didn't muster out here when most of the regiment did."

"What does muster mean?"

"It's a military word. Means to gather troops. They're mustered when they're formed and they're mustered for pay, sick call and when they're disbanded. Your boy might possibly have run off too . . . skedaddled was the word used for that" — Rose did not think Will would have skedaddled — "but they may have been ill or wounded and, of course, they may have been killed. The 81st fought in some of the war's worst battles after February '64. They were at Cold Harbor and lost two thirds of their number there. They were at Petersburg, Chaffin's Bluff, and the siege of the Confederate capital at Richmond. They took a terrible beating. Your aunt can find the details of those battles in any history of the Civil War but you can give her this." He handed Rose a booklet titled *Oswego County in the Civil War*. "There's a lot of useful information in it. And tell her to get in touch with me if she needs anything more. Would you like to take along a photocopy of the names?"

She left Mr. Ancaster's office, her head full of the things he had told her, with the photocopy that said

Will Morrissay had joined the Union Army in Oswego in 1864 held tight in her hand. She walked for some time, trying to imagine the town as it had been for Will. She sat down on a low stone wall and looked at the photocopy with Will's name. Then she took the scrap of a song out of her pocket. She unwrapped it carefully, studying the notes she could not read.

"What's that song?"

Rose went cold, and crammed the song back in her pocket. Sam was standing in front of her, his hands behind his back.

"I didn't see you." Rose swallowed hard, trying not to show her nervousness.

"Can I sit down?"

"It's not my wall."

Sam didn't move. "I'm sorry," he said abruptly.

"What for? That this isn't my wall?"

"No, I'm sorry I've been such a pig to you."

Rose looked up at him for a second. His face was almost as red as his hair and he was gazing steadfastly at his feet.

"Oh, well, I . . . ." Rose was trying to say with careless disdain, "I haven't noticed that you've been a pig," but her voice started to croak and she couldn't get the words out. Sam's apology was so unexpected.

"This is what happened," said Sam, still not looking at her. "Mother and I were going to Italy — to Florence — so I could look at paintings and sculpture. She promised me we could go, ages ago, one time when I won a prize for a painting. She said if she ever got a big chunk of money all at once she'd take me and ever since then I've read all sorts of books about Florence. Then this spring she won a prize and some money for a book she wrote, and she said we could go in the fall. She said it would be the best time, when all the other tourists were back home. I could stay out of school and we could go for a month. On purpose she didn't start another book. Then your grandmother died and your aunt what's-her-name phoned and said could you come and live with us and Mom said, yes, of course. She said she couldn't very well say you could come then take right off for Florence. So we used the money to fix up the kitchen and some other things — and I was mad. I guess I've been really rotten. Yesterday when you threw up in the ditch, first I thought you were awful then I thought what if it was me. So I started thinking about how mean I'd been to say those things. And anyway, I didn't mean to say them where you could hear and . . . well, I'm sorry, that's all."

Rose had never before been the cause of someone having to do without something really important. For her, going to Italy wasn't anything special, but she could see that for Sam it was a dream. Having been kept for three weeks from going back to Will and Susan, she knew the pain of that kind of disappointment.

"I can see why you hate me," she said. "I'd hate me if I really wanted to go some place and I came along and wouldn't let me.''

"I don't hate you. Not any more anyhow.''

"It's all right. I mean I'm glad if you don't hate me any more, but I know you can't like me either. I don't mind.''

"What do you mean? Why can't I like you?''

"Nobody does.''

"That's dumb. People like you.''

"No they don't.''

"I do.''

"No you don't.''

"I don't?''

"No. Nobody does. It's because I don't belong here.''

"Don't belong here? What do you mean?'' Sam had got over his awkwardness. He sat down on the stone wall beside Rose.

"I don't belong here,'' she repeated. "I figured it out a long time ago. I . . . .'' She stopped and looked down at her hands, her fingers nervously entwined. Sam's sudden, unexpected offer of friendship had filled her with an overpowering rush of gratitude and an immediate urge to confide in him — to give him something in return. "I . . . Sam, if I tell you something, will you promise not to tell anyone else?''

"Sure.''

"Do you promise?''

"I promise.''

Rose told him the story of Mrs. Morrissay, the root cellar and Susan and Will. Then she showed him the photocopy of Will's name and took the crumpled song out of her pocket and showed him that.

Sam got up. He paced back and forth in front of her,

his hands first swinging wildly at his sides, then pushing through his hair until it stood on end like the quills of a porcupine. Finally he stopped in front of her. "O.K." he said, "I admit I thought I saw a ghost that one morning and I admit it did look like an old lady" — he swallowed — "in fact sort of like the old lady you're talking about, and it wasn't just a silhouette. I only said that to steer Mom off. It was a face and everything but it *could* have been shadows and so could yours. All that other stuff about the root cellar and going back in time — that's crazy. But even if it were absolutely true it wouldn't mean you belonged there — you belong here. You belong with us. You're our cousin. Even if you are an American." Sam grinned. "But that's O.K. My mother's an American too, remember? Your father was my mother's brother. His name was David Larkin, and there's a picture of him on my mother's dresser. I'll show you when we get home. I don't know why you think people don't like you. Why shouldn't they unless" — Sam came to a halt in front of Rose — "unless it's because you don't like the rest of us very much. You're not exactly the friendliest person in the world, you know."

Sam stopped. Rose said nothing. She was too stunned. David Larkin — she had never thought about her father as a real person, someone who might even be in a photograph, someone other people knew about. She felt a curious sense of shock. "Come on," she heard Sam saying, "it's getting cold, let's go find something to eat. How much money have you got?"

Rose searched her pockets and found a couple of dollars and some change. She got up from the wall and together they walked down the hill. Sam asked if she would show him Will's song and he played it on his harmonica as they walked.

Prickles stood out on the back of Rose's neck and along her arms, listening to Sam play Will's song. She stopped and closed her eyes and put her hands tightly to her face trying to hold the world still, so swiftly did it seem to spin and whirl. Through the notes Rose heard again in her head the sharp sweet tones of the wood thrush. Sam stopped and looked at her in alarm. "Your face is white as paper. Are you O.K.?"

"Yes." Rose clenched and unclenched her hands in her pockets and in a moment she felt better. After a few minutes she began to hum the song, thinking about Will and about her unknown father.

Eventually they found themselves on what looked to be an old street that ran along the water. It was lined with weathered buildings, most of them crooked and leaning against each other as though seeking comfort against the wind that even on this balmy day carried with it a chill from the lake. There were shops along one side, and a cheerful-looking restaurant with a geranium in the window invited them to come inside. They ate muffins and drank cider together. Sam told Rose what he knew of her father, which was only that Aunt Nan had loved him very much. Rose listened, bemused. Then she tried to explain to him about her own life in great cities around the world.

"No wonder you think nobody likes you," said Sam after a while, "if the only people you know are those aunts and uncles. You don't know any people, not kids, not ordinary people. You're just lucky your father had a sister and she had kids and they're us.''

''I guess so,'' said Rose, but she was too confused in her mind to think clearly about that or any of what Sam had said that afternoon. It had upset everything she'd always thought true and it was rather wonderful but she didn't trust it. In fact she didn't really believe that Sam didn't hate her.

But all the way home the next day, Rose thought about what Sam had said, and she felt the beginning of a warm feeling inside her.

When they arrived, Aunt Nan was waiting for them.

THE ACCIDENT

The car had hardly stopped in the driveway before Aunt Nan was out through the kitchen door and across the yard. Rose got out to meet her, knowing she was going to be scolded. She was not prepared for the hurt and rage that greeted her.

Aunt Nan's face was white and her eyes were red and swollen. She was in a greater state of disarray than Rose had ever seen her. Her hair looked like an owl's nest, her skirt was hanging way down at the back where she had not done it up properly and her sweater was on inside out.

"You must be the most difficult child the world has ever known," she said in low, angry, carefully measured tones. "You're ungrateful, inconsiderate, selfish and cruel. After your Uncle Bob phoned on Thursday I could hardly believe my ears. You knew it was a special outing. I told you so myself. Are you so used to doing absolutely everything you want that you had to go skulking in the back of the station wagon to ruin the trip for Sam and George and Uncle Bob? And all you left me was this. I would never have found it if I hadn't started to feel sorry for you. I went upstairs this morning to get your dirty laundry and there it was!''

There were tears in Aunt Nan's eyes by this time, and she shoved a piece of paper under Rose's nose that Rose recognized as her monogrammed stationery — the letter she had written to Aunt Millicent and never sent. She had forgotten all about it.

''Can you imagine how I felt?'' Aunt Nan had lost her careful control and her voice was rising with every word. ''Can you just imagine? Well, Miss Rose Larkin, I'll tell you what I did. I went straight to the phone and called your Aunt Millicent and she was very upset. She said she couldn't imagine what had gotten into you. She said she didn't know what to do. She'd have to talk to Arnold and Stella and phone me back. I don't know what to do with you. I've never been so upset in my whole life. But you can just be sure someone will find you a nice orphanage *somewhere*!''

Aunt Nan had run out of steam. Tears were pouring down her face and she was gripping Rose's arm as though Rose were a wild animal fighting to get loose. But Rose stood still, utterly shaken. She hardly felt the pain of Aunt Nan's frenzied grip. She couldn't speak.

''Nan, Nan, what's this all about?'' demanded Uncle Bob. ''Let me see that paper.'' He loosened Aunt Nan's fingers from the now crumpled, tear-soaked paper. The boys stood in awed silence. Aunt Nan let go of Rose's arm and reached for her handkerchief. Rose thought she was going to hit her and leaped back in fright. She slipped, fell, picked herself up and in a panic started to run towards the back of the house. All she could think of was the safety of the root cellar.

"No, you don't," cried Aunt Nan, "you're not running off. You can just stay right here and face the music, you little coward" — and she lunged after her. She ran a few steps, slid on a patch of wet leaves, her feet went out from under her, and she fell flat on her back. For a moment nobody moved. Then Uncle Bob was kneeling beside her. "Rose," murmured Aunt Nan and fainted.

"Call the doctor," barked Uncle Bob. White faced, Sam ran into the house. Aunt Nan opened her eyes.

"Thank God," said Uncle Bob. "Now lie absolutely still. I don't think you should move until Dr. Best gets here."

The twins had started to cry and George was angrily telling them to shut up. Rose, halfway to the corner of the house, had turned and in anguish watched the scene as though it were happening at a great distance. George turned to glare murderously at her but otherwise no one paid her any attention.

Dr. Best was not long getting there. She looked Aunt Nan over carefully, felt for broken bones, got her to stand up, and with Uncle Bob's help led her into the house.

After she had gone George turned on Rose. "Are you crazy or something?" he yelled. "You could've killed Mom. You're the most selfish person in the whole world!"

The twins stared from Rose to George and back again, their faces solemn, their eyes big and round and frightened. Sam came out through the door.

"Come on, you guys," he said to the twins. "Mom's O.K. The doctor's in there talking to her and I heard them laughing. You want to play race cars? You come too,'' he turned towards Rose.

"No," said Rose hoarsely.

"Come on," he said, coming over to her. "It wasn't your fault. Mom gets like that sometimes — she goes hairy. That's all this is. The doctor says she's O.K. Come on."

"No."

"Well, all right, but — all right." Sam went inside the house. With one withering look, George followed them.

"She's going to die," Rose whispered to herself. "She's going to die and the baby's going to die and it's my fault." She had not moved from where she had stopped half an hour before, when Aunt Nan had fallen. She could not move, her legs would not carry her. The scene replayed itself in her mind — the shouts and shrieks, her breaking loose from Aunt Nan's clutch, Aunt Nan running after her and the fall, over and over again, the fall.

The doctor came out of the house. At last Rose moved.

"Please," she said, "is Aunt Nan going to die?"

"Oh, no, of course not," said Dr. Best. She was a small, sturdy woman who in her brisk movements exuded a sense of confidence. "No, she's going to be fine, the baby's going to be fine. The only problem is that she's wrenched her back and she's going to have to stay in bed for at least a month. As long as she's careful she'll be fine. You'll all have to help. Don't you worry."

"Thank you, thank you very much," said Rose, and without stopping to say goodbye she ran around the corner of the house and threw herself to the ground beside the root cellar doors.

"I don't care," she said again and again to herself. "She's all right and I didn't kill her. She hates me but she's going to be all right, I didn't kill her. Sam's wrong. I don't belong here. I don't."

She was so consumed by her own misery that she almost let the shadow of the thorn tree slip past the opening between the doors. Just in time she jumped up and ran down the steps.

WHEN THE WIND
COMES UP

Rose sniffed the summer air hungrily. But she didn't have the strength of spirit to go looking for Susan. Instead, she sat down and clasped her hands tightly around her knees and put her head down. The words still pounded in her head: "ungrateful, inconsiderate, selfish, cruel." "You could've killed Mom." Then she heard again Sam's voice, "not exactly the friendliest person in the world, you know." She shuddered and tried to push the voices out of her mind but still they hammered at her. "I didn't kill her," she whispered. "I'm not going back there ever, if I get to be three hundred and seventy-five years old. Never!"

"Rose?" said Susan's soft voice, "Rose, are you sick?"

Rose looked up. "Oh, Susan," she said and, for the first time she could ever remember, she burst into tears. "I did something really awful and Aunt Nan almost died." Through her tears she told Susan what had happened.

When she had finished there was a silence that to

Rose seemed filled with her shame and unkindness. Then Susan said, "Well, I don't see you been so terrible bad. I don't suppose you ought to have stowed away in the cart but it ain't such a terrible thing. The letter was too bad. You wrote it when you was mad. You can see how it would be a hard thing to come across. And besides, your aunt's pregnant and sometimes that makes a person chancy. Even cats and cows when they're pregnant can be some upset. Not that you have to be pregnant to have a chancy temper. I guess you ain't used to hearing people get riled like that. From what you say, your gran never did."

"No, she didn't."

"Well, it seems to me your aunt is one who does. You'll get used to it. When you go back there you'll feel lots better."

"I'm not going back. Ever!"

"Oh, Rose, of course you will! Them folk's good. You'll catch on to how to get on with 'em." Susan pushed back a strand of her bright brown hair and smiled.

Rose sighed quaveringly. Susan's soothing voice and kind words at least restored her to calm. She remembered why she had come. She fished into the pocket of her jeans for Will's song and handed it to Susan. "Did it work?" she asked eagerly. "How long have I been gone?"

"It's a week since you come last."

Rose breathed a happy sigh. "It's a week for me, too."

Susan gave the song back to Rose. "You better keep it for now. Will said you brought good luck when he wanted so bad to talk to the birds. And it worked to bring you now so mebbe, if you keep it, it will bring us both luck, and Will too.''

"Then you keep my rose." Rose put the song back in her pocket. "Susan, I saw Will's name on a list in Oswego." She told her about Mr. Ancaster and Fort Ontario.

Susan had only one thing to say. "He didn't find no list that said when they come back."

"No, but he said that didn't mean they didn't come. It only means they didn't come when most of the others did. Susan, what we have to do is go to Oswego and find out."

The idea had sailed into Rose's head so swiftly and neatly that she had hardly time to notice it before the words were out. "I had a booklet but I left it in the car with the copy of the list. It told where all the battles were. I can remember quite a lot of them. But we can find out more if we go over to the fort again. They'll know. And we can go to see Stephen Jerue's family."

"Rose, we can't do that!"

"Why not?"

"It's too far."

"It isn't. I've been there. I've just come back from there."

"I never been farther than Soames. I can't go."

"Susan, what if Will is sick or wounded and can't get home and can't let us know, and they could tell us at the fort where to look. Maybe Stephen Jerue is home already and he can tell us."

Susan looked doubtful.

"What if not going means we never see Will again?"

"I'll go," said Susan. Her eyes were large and fearful.

She clasped and unclasped her hands nervously. "I'll go," she repeated. "But whatever's the missus going to say?"

"It's for Will, isn't it? We'll go across Lake Ontario on one of those schooners and we'll find the Jerues. I'm sure they'll help us. Then we'll find —— Susan, we don't have any money!"

"I got some."

"Go get it."

Although she was now three years younger than Susan, Rose suddenly realized that she, not Susan, knew what had to be done this time. She knew that she had to take charge now or they would never leave Hawthorn Bay, never find Will, never be able to face any danger or difficulty that might lie ahead. It was as though Susan, too, understood. She hesitated for a moment then ran off into the house.

She was gone long enough for the last of the afternoon to fade into evening. An oriole trilling his three liquid notes flitted higher and higher into the shadowy leaves of the big maple tree. A chipmunk scurried along the rail fence that separated the garden from the rest of the backyard. Susan came out of the kitchen. Her face was stiff and white. Her mouth was set in a straight line. "Will's ma's raising an awful ruckus, crying and carrying on about how Will wouldn't never have gone if it wasn't for Steve's bad influence. As if anyone could make Will Morrissay do a thing he hadn't the mind to."

"Does that mean you won't go?"

"I'm coming and, what's more, I made her give me five Yankee dollars." Susan opened her fist and showed Rose a handful of money. "And I got more. At the bottom of my trunk. Forty dollars — Yankee too. Ma and Pa saved it from their wedding trip in the States and left it for me to get married with but I figure mebbe this is more important.''

''Then we can go. All we have to do is get a ride on a ship.''

''First thing in the morning we can go on up to Jamie Heaton's. Like as not they've got a load going to Oswego. Rose would you mind saying you was a boy, like me and Will thought the first time we saw you?''

''Why?''

''Well, you know. Boys get paid more mind to and, what's more, I'd be safer.''

''How come?''

''Folks will think I got protection. And, anyway, nobody'd believe you're a girl in them britches and your hair all cut off.''

''All right. I don't care. You can say my name is David.''

Rose slept that night in the barn. She was up and ready when Susan came for her at dawn. Susan had on a blue and white checkered dress and a small black bonnet with a pink flower in it. She looked neat and pretty. She was carrying Rose's overnight bag in one hand and in the other a small square straw one of her own.

Gratefully Rose took her bag. ''I forgot I left it here,'' she said.

They took turns rowing up the bay, eating bread and cheese as they went. They startled a big blue heron away from his breakfast. He gronked crossly at them as he took off, his huge wings pumping up and down like some great prehistoric bird. From somewhere behind them a loon called in his high fluttering tones. "It isn't like any other place in the whole world," sighed Rose. Susan nodded.

Within ten minutes they heard men's voices and soon pulled into sight of a wharf where a small sailing ship was being loaded with grain.

"It's Arn Colliver. I expect he'll take us," said Susan. Her voice was tight and nervous. "Captain Colliver," she called, shipping the oars and tying the boat to the wharf. "If you're going to Oswego, me and my friend — David — want to sail with you." She climbed up onto the wharf. Rose scrambled after. "Will, he ain't come home yet from the war and I figure to go looking for him."

"Well now, Susan Anderson, can you trim a sail?" asked the captain. Without waiting for an answer he walked away from them down the plank into the ship.

"Isn't he going to tell us if we can come?" Rose was worried.

"He'll take us. When the wind comes up." Susan perched tensely on the edge of a large wooden box. Rose followed suit, watching the short bulky figure of Captain Colliver as he moved about on the deck of the ship, overseeing the loading of the grain from the wagons drawn up to the wharf and for half a mile behind. It was a long, low ship with three masts and a single cabin on the deck. The grain was being loaded into the hold below. One by one the wagons were emptied, the farmers "geed hawed" and "giddapped" their horses, leaving the captain, and the three boys and the man who made up his crew, to level the grain.

"That's Billy Foster and Joe Heaton and I don't know

the other boy. Hank Bother's the cook," Susan told Rose. "The two boys belong to our Church. That Billy Foster was an awful one for making trouble when he was a little feller. Him and Will's brother Adam, they was a pair of terrible teasers. If it hadn't of been for Will there's times I might have run off. I come to Morrissays to work when I was nine. Them boys made things miserable for me. I used to hide back in Bothers' woods and Will, he'd come and find me and make Adam leave off."

The sun got hotter and hotter as they talked. Finally, just before noon, a breeze started up and Captain Colliver came out of the cabin. "All right lads," he called. "Looks like a wind's coming up. Let's get going." He shooed away several cats and a large dog and nodded at Rose and Susan. "Come aboard you two."

"This here's David," said Susan. Captain Colliver nodded brusquely but said nothing. "Island folks is like that," Susan told Rose later. "They don't pry into a body's business though they're busting to know things."

The girls went down the gangplank into the schooner and sat down on a coil of rope. With the captain at the wheel giving orders the three boys untied the ropes that held the ship and with long poles pushed away from the wharf. They drifted slowly out into the lake and hoisted a sail. As the wind caught the sail the captain straightened the schooner, the boys hoisted the remaining sails and they were away.

There was the odour of fish, the musty scent of the grain below and the sharp smell of fresh coffee brewing in the cabin. Rose felt the cool wind against her back, lifting the hot hair from her head. She smiled at Susan. Weakly Susan smiled back.

At noon they ate pork and onions and potatoes and rhubarb pie. By this time the neighbour boys had made Susan acquainted with Robert James, an Oswego boy who said he knew Will's cousin Steve. While they ate, Robert spoke of Steve and the other boys who had gone to fight in the war. "The regiments have been coming home since April," he said, with awe in his voice. "We've been having some mighty celebrations for them. The 147th come in July and there wasn't more than a hundred and forty-seven of them to come neither. The 110th ain't home yet."

"What about the 81st?" asked Rose tensely.

"Is that them Steve Jerue went off with? They was the ones that was first into Richmond. They took a company of coloureds with them. It must have been something for them coloured fellers to march into that rebel town and raise the old stars and stripes over it! Boy, I wish I'd been there!"

"What do you mean, 'coloured'?" asked Rose.

"The slaves."

"Oh. Have they come home yet?" Rose persisted.

"I believe they come home only the other day but I ain't talked to any of them yet."

Rose and Susan looked quickly at each other, then as quickly looked away, their eyes saying maybe, maybe, not daring more.

After dinner Susan, who had got over her initial nervousness, insisted that she and Rose help, so they scraped and washed the tin cups and plates.

The voyage took all night. Wrapped in blankets, Rose

and Susan slept on deck. Rose woke once in the night. She heard the water slapping against the sides of the ship and the ropes creaking as they pulled in their blocks. She looked up and saw the immense blue-black sky sprinkled with bright stars and fell back to sleep, wondering if the whole adventure was a dream.

In the morning she woke to find they had reached Oswego harbour. To the east was Fort Ontario, farther in along the waterfront were warehouses and huge grain elevators. In the distance, church spires rose high over the town. The harbour was full of barges, tug boats and sailing ships at anchor.

"Here, give a hand to haul in on this." Robert James threw her an end of rope. Shoulder to shoulder with the boys, she leaned back, her feet apart, and pulled with all her strength as the schooner slid up against the wharf.

After they had docked, Robert offered to guide them to the Jerues. "That's good of you," said Susan gratefully. When she offered passage money to Captain Colliver he pushed her hand aside gently. "Many's the sail I had with Bob Morrissay in his day. I guess I can help out where his boy figures." Susan nodded.

They followed Robert along Water Street where Rose and Sam had had lunch in the restaurant with the pink geranium in the window. The street was crowded. Women wore long, wide hoop skirts, with shawls over their shoulders and straw bonnets on their heads. Men had narrow-legged dark suits, high shirt collars, and on their heads tall silk hats or flat straw ones. Rose was fascinated but there was no time to stop and look. Robert wove his way through the morning crowd of dock workers and shoppers, like a needle darting through cloth. They caught only a glimpse of the coal yards, the starch company, and rows of interesting-looking shops as they flew by.

Robert stopped at the bridge that spanned the river dividing the town. "We had a banquet here," he said proudly. "Right here on the bridge. When the 127th come home. They was so badly done the whole town gave them a banquet. There was near two thousand people all sitting at one long table. It ran the full length of the bridge. My dad says we ain't likely to see anything like it ever again."

They crossed the bridge and walked away from the centre of town up along streets that Rose remembered from her walk with Uncle Bob. She looked over at Susan to tell her and saw Susan's pale, set face. With her eyes she followed where Susan was looking and realized, for the first time, how many soldiers there were. While she had been caught up in the wonder of Oswego and the people in their curious 1865 clothes, Susan had been watching for Will in every face. And she had forgotten. And there were so many — some marching smartly along with a wife or mother, their uniforms fresh and spruce, others in faded uniforms, their faces drawn and hollow-eyed, others without an arm or leg — so many, and she too began to search every face, trembling with the realization that the war over might not mean that Will was all right.

About halfway along a wide, shady street they came to a huge brown clapboard house with a screened porch around it and flowers along its walk.

"Here's Jerues'," said Robert.

"I didn't know they was rich," said Susan in surprise, "it's a big house."

"They keep boarders."

At that moment a woman came out of the house and down the steps, carrying a shopping basket on her arm. She was a tall stout woman with a comfortable kitcheny-looking face. She had on a bright purple flowered dress with a hoop so large the dress stuck out at least a foot and a half from her body all around. On her head was a large yellow straw bonnet decorated with velvet daisies and bright red cherries. "You looking for someone?" she asked.

"We've come to find Will Morrissay," said Rose.

"Will?"

"I'm Susan Anderson, Mrs. Jerue." Susan stepped forward nervously. "You know me. I works for Morrissays over to Hawthorn Bay in Canada."

"My land, child! Of course I know you. What on earth are you doing here?"

"We've come to find Will," repeated Rose.

"Will?" said Mrs. Jerue in bewilderment. "Why are you looking for Will? Where's he gone?"

"We thought since Will and your son Steve joined the army together maybe they came home together?"

A group of children had collected on the sidewalk. Robert James said goodbye and went off. Nobody noticed.

"You mean to say that my nephew Will Morrissay went and joined up? And never said a word about it, and Stevie neither? Not even in one of his letters? Oh, my land. It must have nearly killed his mother."

"Ain't they here?" asked Susan faintly.

"There, now." Mrs. Jerue put her arms around Susan and hugged her tightly. "The war's been an awful grief to us all. We had letters regular up to February then they stopped. The regiment come home last week and the adjutant says there's boys still to come who've been wounded or took sick or had special duties with another regiment. He says Steve took sick, and that he got a wound. But'' — her voice faltered — ''he couldn't tell me nothing more. I didn't know, of course, to ask about Will — oh, imagine those boys doing that and not telling a soul. Anyway he said he was sorry to say he hadn't seen hide nor hair of Steve since they was in Richmond — come to think of it now I recall he said 'those boys' but I didn't pay much mind at the time. Then he said we'd have to wait, that's all we can do and, my sweet lamb, that's all I can tell you.'' Mrs. Jerue took a large handkerchief from her sleeve and wiped away a tear.

''We won't wait,'' said Rose. ''We came here to find Will. If he's in Richmond we'll have to go there.''

''Oh, no, son, you can't go to Richmond!'' Mrs. Jerue was aghast. ''Why Richmond's away down south hundreds of miles from here and what's more, it's all burned out. I suppose you don't hear about those things across the lake. The rebels burned out the city the night before our soldiers marched in. And there's sickness and desperate people. Desperate people all through the south I daresay. You can't go down there by yourself, a delicate little fellow like you.''

''Not by myself,'' said Rose firmly. ''Susan and I are going together.''

''Well, now.'' Mrs. Jerue was somewhat taken aback. ''You're a right forward little mite, aren't you? What's your name, son?''

''David Larkin. I come from New York City. I . . . I ran away when my father and brothers were killed in the war and my mother had to go out to work. But the war's over now and Susan said she'd take me home.''

"I must say you're a plucky little fellow. You can't be too much older than Charlie here." Mrs. Jerue put her hand on the curly brown head of a boy standing beside her. He looked to be about eight.

"I'm twelve," declared Rose.

"Land sakes! Aren't you something! Your mother will be in a state over you. She's lost all those boys and for all she knows she's lost you too. You oughtn't to have run off like that. Well, there's trains every day to New York and there'll be no trick to finding someone going there who'll take you along and see you find your mother. For now you just stay with us. And Susan, you'll have to go on home. Who brought you over?''

"Arn Colliver.''

"Arn don't usually stay more than a day so you can likely go back with him in the morning. Come along inside the both of you now and have a wash-up and a bite to eat.''

Rose had not figured on Mrs. Jerue being difficult. "We can't go back yet," she insisted stubbornly. "We have to find Will. We need to go see that captain you talked to at the fort.''

"I declare I never saw the likes of you!" Mrs. Jerue put her hands on her hips and blinked down at Rose. "You can't go to Richmond, son. I'd never sleep a wink nights worrying about you. It's bad enough in the north with soldiers on the loose all over the countryside — oh my, no, the good Lord wouldn't give me a minute's peace if I let you go. But I don't suppose there's any harm in you going on up to the fort to talk to Captain

Prentiss if it'll settle your minds. After dinner, Charlie here can show you the way."

Huffing and puffing from heat and exertion, Mrs. Jerue led the way into the house. The children Rose had taken for neighbours turned out to be the seven small Jerue boys. Whispering and staring, careful not to miss a thing that was going on, they followed. A small, fat cocker spaniel waddled after.

"And you keeps boarders along with all these young ones?" Susan was incredulous.

"Oh my, yes. The children fit neat as pins into the spare corners and the men don't mind at all. They're mostly sailors from over your way. Mother kept boarders before me, that's how Bob Morrissay come to marry my sister Patty and took her off to Canada."

As she talked Mrs. Jerue squeezed herself down a narrow hall and into a large sunny kitchen at the back of the house. It was a big square room with a large scrubbed wooden table in the middle. Between the tall windows at the back was a big black wood stove. To the right of it was a stairway and a pantry beyond. It reminded Rose of old Tom Bother's kitchen without the clutter.

"Now you" — Mrs. Jerue set her shopping basket on the table — "you get along to the washroom and wash up the dirt. Outhouse is out back if you need it." She took off her bonnet and shook out her fading blond ringlets. She turned to the stairway and shouted in a voice that would have served a drill sergeant well, "Girls!"

Feet pounded. Three girls, from about nine to fourteen years of age, in dresses made from the same blue cloth with white pinafores over them, came down the stairs.

"Sally, Jenny, Louisa, this is Susan Anderson from your Aunt Patty's across the lake. It's a while since you been there, you may not remember Susan." The girls all smiled. "And this here's David."

In fifteen minutes, under their mother's watchful supervision, the girls had put a meal on the table: enormous plates of cold chicken, potato salad, lettuce, tomatoes, fresh rolls, and fresh peaches with cream so thick Mrs. Jerue had to spoon it on. She said a quick blessing, the children scraped their chairs, nudged each other, shushed each other loudly and giggled throughout the meal. The cocker spaniel watched every mouthful eagerly, obviously expecting a share.

"Well, now, I expect it will set Patty's mind more at rest too if you was to go up to the fort and talk to Captain Prentiss." Mrs. Jerue got up from the table. "Charlie," she said. Gleefully Charlie detached himself from the group. "Follow me," he commanded.

The day was sultry. There was no breeze and people were walking slowly, some of them fanning themselves with newspapers or fans. Charlie marched along smartly while Rose and Susan kept pace half a block behind.

"She's right," said Susan anxiously. "Richmond's too far for us."

"No it isn't." Rose put her hand in her pocket and pulled out Will's song. "This is for good luck, remember? We'll get there and we'll find Will."

"It ain't no use. It's too far. We shouldn't have come."

Rose firmly began to hum Will's song.

The fort was a confusion of tired-looking soldiers in blue uniforms. There were soldiers everywhere, lounging on the grass, walking around, standing on duty. The air smelled of sweat and horses.

Charlie presented himself to the sentry. "I want to see Captain Prentiss. I'm Stevie Jerue's brother."

"That so, sonny?" the sentry smiled. "Well, we got a lot of brothers here and we're pretty busy getting them sorted out. We got no time for kids, so how's about you just running along now?"

Rose pushed her way forward. "We have to see Captain Prentiss. We've come all the way across the lake. It's important."

"Please," said Susan.

"Sorry." The sentry was firm.

Rose was not to be thwarted. She opened her mouth and shouted, "Captain Prentiss! Captain Prentiss!"

"Now that's enough!" The sentry was no longer smiling. "You just get yourselves ——"

"Wait a minute, sonny. Captain Prentiss is right over there. Wait here." A soldier standing inside the gate had been listening to them. He went over to a group on the far side of the parade square and spoke to a tall officer. Together they came back to the gate.

"Yes, I'm John Prentiss. What can I do for you?" the captain asked Susan.

"We're looking for Will Morrissay," said Rose.

Suddenly the captain looked very tired. Rose felt a pang of fear. Beside her Susan drew in her breath sharply.

"I see," said the captain. He looked down at Charlie.

"And what's your name?"

"Charles Walker Jerue."

"I see." Captain Prentiss looked at Rose again. Susan couldn't stand it any longer. "Is Will dead?" she whispered.

"I don't know," said the captain. "I really don't know. The last time I saw either of those boys was in Richmond outside the Libby prison as the flag was going up. Things got pretty disorganized for a while after that, and by the time we had ourselves sorted out those boys had disappeared. I don't know what happened to them. I'm sorry."

" 'Scuse me, Captain." It was the soldier who had spoken up for them before, a short, red-bearded man.

"Yes, Christie?"

"I couldn't help hearing what you was saying and I wanted to tell these kids that I knowed both them boys and there ain't no one in the Union army could have called either of 'em a skedaddler. I seen Steve wounded at Cold Harbor and he never once stopped to think about it through the whole battle and when he took sick Will was like a nurse to him."

"Was — was Will hurt?" Susan's face was pale.

"No, no he wasn't hurt, not so far as I remember. Could be, you know, they got separated from the rest of us at Richmond. Steve was pretty sick."

"It's possible that they attached themselves to another regiment," said Captain Prentiss. "The only thing we can do is wait to find out. I'm sorry."

"If they took sick where would they be?" Susan's voice shook.

"Well, it would likely be in Washington — but, see

here, you youngsters can't go down there by yourselves!'' Captain Prentiss was thunderstruck.

"Mister, if them boys is lying in some hospital
needing care I expect there's no way for us to know
about it without we go and find out.'' Susan's eyes
flashed. Rose could hardly believe it was Susan suddenly so bold.

Captain Prentiss told them it would be impossible for
them to go to Washington. "A young girl with only a little boy for protection. It's a long, expensive, tiring
journey. There's almost no chance of finding the lads. If
they're in a hospital in Washington they'll be sent home
as soon as they can walk. And if . . . .'' Captain Prentiss
did not finish his sentence. Instead he said gently, "I'm
afraid you really will have to wait like the rest of us.''
He wished them well and went back across the green.

"They were a good pair of lads,'' said Christie sadly to
himself, and followed the captain.

Susan was badly shaken by what Captain Prentiss had
said.

"That's what he told Ma,'' said Charlie. "Go home
and wait. Ma says it's no use hanging around the train
station like some folks do. You want to go down to the
ball field?'' he asked Rose. "Or go swimming?''

"No thank you.'' Rose was busy thinking. Charlie offered one or two more suggestions, gave up, and as soon
as they reached the foot of his street, he took off.

"We'll take the train,'' announced Rose when Charlie
was out of earshot. "Mrs. Jerue says they go every day.
We'll go to Washington. But first we have to talk her
into not sending you home.''

But Mrs. Jerue would not hear of it. No matter what

they said, no matter how they pleaded.

"Arn Colliver's gone already," she told Susan, "but Jake Pierson from your bay is going in the morning. As for you, young David, you stay here by me until I can find somebody going to New York City. Now then Susan, as long as you're here you might as well give my girls a hand at getting supper for the men. You run along with the boys, David. Mind, no mischief."

Rose had only one thing in mind. Looking carefully in all directions to make sure she was not being observed, she sauntered towards the bottom of the street and around the corner. She asked the first person she saw for directions to the railroad station. Then she ran.

The station was a big barn of a building with tall dusty windows all around. At one end of the room were high-backed benches in rows; at the other end the ticket seller was reading a newspaper behind a wicket. The station was otherwise deserted. Standing on tiptoe to make herself seen, Rose asked what time the train went to Washington and how much it cost. "Eight o'clock, same as always," answered the ticket seller, not looking up from his newspaper. "Change at Syracuse, Albany and New York City. Fare's thirteen dollars and eighty five cents."

"Is it eight in the morning or eight at night?"

"Eight in the morning. You get to New York at seven-thirty p.m. Connections to Washington at twelve midnight."

When Rose arrived back at the Jerues the boarders had been fed and the family was sitting down to a meal larger than the one they had eaten at noon.

After dinner Mrs. Jerue said, "Well, it's all arranged

with Jake Pierson. He says to be down to the wharf by half past seven and if the wind's come up good he'll sail.''

Susan said, ''Yes, ma'am,'' obediently, and went upstairs to the little room they had been given to sleep in.

''Now you children brighten up them long faces,'' Mrs. Jerue told them as she bid them goodnight. ''You'd think tomorrow was hanging day for the both of you. It ain't. Susan's going home where she's needed and you're going home where I'm sure your mother is going to be one mighty happy woman. I know it's a trial but you have to have some faith that our boys will get home safe without your help. The good Lord's been running this old world a long time without your telling him how to do it and I wouldn't be one bit surprised if he was to go on doing it long after you're both pushing up the daisies.''

After she had left them they looked the room over for a means of escape. All that offered itself was one window with a porch roof below but the porch was at least twelve feet down, and there was another twelve or thirteen feet from there to the ground. It seemed as though Mrs. Jerue had known what they meant to do. The only entrance to the room was through her bedroom.

They sat for over an hour concocting wild plans. Sitting on their cots they talked in whispers of tying sheets together and lowering themselves out of the window. Susan was sure they would fall and break all their bones. Rose said that even if they managed to get away and hide all night in the railroad station, Mrs. Jerue was sure to discover they had gone.

''She'll come marching down to the station to get us.'' Rose giggled. ''I can see them, the seven little boys, the three girls and maybe all the boarders too. 'Give up the girls!' they'll shout, then they'll lead us off in chains.''

"What if we set out for the schooner without making no fuss and then slip off and go to the train?"

"Susan! You're a genius! Why didn't I think of that?"

"Shhh!"

"All right. What we have to do is say I'm coming to see you off. Then we'll get away somehow and get over to the station. I wish I hadn't made up that story about New York then we could both go without them asking why. Mrs. Jerue said you have to be at the wharf at seven-thirty, so if we run like thieves we can get the train on time. What a great idea!"

Susan smiled. "Ain't you getting giddy. I never knowed you to be like this. Like Min Jerue says, you're a forward little fellow."

"Yes, I am, aren't I!" Rose was pleased with how things were working out. She had never before felt so in command of a situation in her life. As Susan said, she felt giddy. "Here, you find room for my things in your suitcase so they won't suspect."

Susan put Rose's socks, underwear and clean jeans in the suitcase with her few things but when Rose handed her the music box and the book she stopped. "What did you bring these for?"

"I don't know," Rose was embarrassed. "I just always do." Susan stuffed Rose's treasures into the corners of her suitcase and said no more about them.

At quarter to seven the next morning, resplendent in a parrot-green dress, Mrs. Jerue served them a breakfast of porridge, ham, eggs and fresh muffins.

"Charlie'll take you down to the wharf," she told

them. "I've made up a package of things I want you to take to Patty and I've written a letter, if you'll oblige, Susan."

"Yes, ma'am." Susan didn't look at Rose.

"I'm going with Charlie to see Susan off," said Rose.

Mrs. Jerue eyed her suspiciously. Rose returned her gaze without blinking. Mrs. Jerue was not convinced. "You go along but mind you stay close by Charlie. Joey says you was down street by yourself yesterday and I'm not sure what you've been up to. I've half a mind to come along and make sure Susan gets off without you."

Rose gulped. She thought quickly. "Why don't you come?" she said sweetly.

"Aw, come on, Ma," said Charlie. "You're too fat, you'll take too long." Nimbly he jumped to avoid the cuff his mother aimed at his right ear.

"Charles Jerue you mind your tongue. Well, it is getting late and I have things to do. You'll have to go without me. But mind, no hanky-panky, David, and I'll see you back here in no more than half an hour. Goodbye, Susan." She gave Susan a hug. "You go on home and be a comfort to poor dear Patty — Lord knows she needs it."

Susan said goodbye and off they went after Charlie who, with some sense of either duty or companionship, stuck right with them until in desperation Rose said loudly, "Oh, Susan, you forgot your shawl!"

"My shawl?" said Susan blankly.

"You *know*, Susan. You left it in the bedroom. If Charlie could run back. . . ."

"Why don't you go yourself?" demanded Charlie.

"I might get lost."

"It's just around the corner. You can't get lost."

Susan looked from one to the other. "Please Charlie," she said in a low voice.

"Oh, all right but you wait. Don't you move."

As soon as Charlie was out of sight Rose grabbed Susan's hand and they raced off.

The station was crowded with people laden with parcels and suitcases, saying goodbyes, chasing straying children. "I'll get the tickets. You keep a lookout in case someone comes after us." Rose's voice was sharp with excitement.

"I ain't standing over here if you're going over there," cried Susan. She grabbed Rose's arm. "Not if Min Jerue and the whole United States army was to come after me, I ain't." So they went together, pushing their way through the crowd, turning anxiously every other second to check if there was anyone coming after them. Waiting in line for the tickets seemed to take forever. Susan was horrified at the cost. "You can buy a whole cow for less than that back home!" But she gave Rose the money.

The train was smaller than any Rose had ever seen. The engine was bright blue and trimmed with brass. It bore a brass bell in front of its cab, and a cow catcher out in front. Its smokestack was cone shaped, the smoke coming out of it in steady puffs. Behind the engine was the coal tender and a row of luggage cars and coaches that proclaimed on their sides: OSWEGO AND SYRACUSE RAILWAY.

Inside, the coach was panelled in dark wood and the seats were straw covered and prickly. Rose and Susan found seats about halfway down the car, stowed their suitcase in the rack overhead and sat down, peering nervously through the window and down the aisle.

The car filled quickly. A woman with four children settled her family in two double seats across the aisle. A sour-looking man, carefully dusting off his seat first, sat down in front of them. A sad-faced soldier, a couple of noisy boys and a very fat woman paraded towards the back of the car. Rose breathed a sigh of relief and sat back just as Susan gasped. ''Look, Rose!'' Through the window Rose saw Charlie coming through the crowd accompanied by a tall man, and followed by Mrs. Jerue steaming like the locomotive, her collar undone and her bonnet awry. As though on signal, Susan and Rose ducked below the window ledge, staring into each other's eyes.

''All aboard'' shouted the conductor. ''All aboard for Syracuse, Albany, New York. All aboard, boooard!''

''Wait!'' It was Mrs. Jerue. ''Wait!''

The train whistled its loud, high-pitched toot-toot, and with a jerk, a stop, and another jerk, pulled out of the station.

THE TRAIN
TO NEW YORK

In a few minutes the conductor came along and punched their tickets. "You youngsters have to change trains at Syracuse," he told them. "Now I'll keep an eye on you and see you get off all right, but you keep Syracuse in mind." He was a big comfortable-looking man with a pink, clean-shaven face and a ready smile, and at first they were grateful to him. But when every time he came through the car he said, "Well, now, how're you youngsters getting on?" and patted Rose on the head, they began to see him as a big nuisance. Rose drew a picture of him in the coal dust on the window, and Susan said he looked a little like a pig Henry Bother had once won a prize for at the Soames fair, that was called Derrington Halpenny. So they called the conductor Derrington Halpenny and nudged each other every time he came near.

They watched through the window as they flew by the farms and villages. Sometimes there were shacks built near the tracks and children came running to line up and wave at the train. Sometimes they passed over brooks or small rivers where the shrill screech of the sawmills could be heard even over the sound of the train.

"They got elms and maples and cedar and tamarack swamps same as us," said Susan. "They got villages that looks like Collivers' Corners even if they talk different and are going all the time. I guess mebbe the States isn't all that different." Comforted by this observation, she settled back.

Rose nodded. "I suppose Americans *are* a lot busier than Canadians."

She watched the woman across the aisle trying to keep her children in order. "I've got to say I'm going to be some pleased to get them home," she called to Rose. It turned out that the woman was called Mrs. Heilbrunner. She was small, with pale skin, pale hair and pale blue eyes. She was dressed in black, because her husband had been killed in the war, and she said she was going to live with her mother and father on the family farm a few miles north of Albany.

Rose told her that she and Susan were brother and sister and they were going south to look for their brother who hadn't come home from the war.

"God bless you." Mrs. Heilbrunner had tears in her eyes. She asked which regiment Will was in. When Rose told her, she exclaimed, "Why, my Walter, Lord rest his soul, was in that regiment. He died at Cold Harbor. What's your brother's name?"

Rose told her about Will and Mrs. Heilbrunner remembered her husband writing her about a boy who could play the flute. "Charm the birds out of the trees he could, that's what my Walter said. And he's your brother, land sake!"

Mrs. Heilbrunner was sympathetic. She told Rose that Walter had been in hospital in Washington and gave her the name of the hospital. Rose wrote it down on the back of her train timetable.

It took four hours to get from Oswego to Syracuse by which time the delight of travelling had begun to wear off. Rose and Susan were sticky from heat and coal dust and glad to change trains just to have something to do. They had no chance to look around the station, however, as Derrington Halpenny took them completely in charge, carrying their suitcase, beaming at them, telling them at every step, "Now you two youngsters, don't you worry. I'll get you on that train for Albany all right." He piloted them through the station and settled them on the Albany train, with three quarters of an hour to wait before it started.

The fat woman and the sour-faced man got on too. Mrs. Heilbrunner and her four children sat down opposite them. A drunk sat right behind them muttering and complaining and drinking noisily out of a bottle he had with him.

Through the window they watched the busy crowds. There were many soldiers and the number of black people amazed Susan. "I ain't never seen but two before," she whispered. "They come across the lake with Captain Armitage. They'd run off from being slaves. They was kind of sad. I don't know where they went after. Ain't they black!"

"I suppose so. I've never thought about it. There are lots of black people in New York, as many as white people, I think. Susan, let's get something to drink."

"We don't need nothing. We got to watch our money.

I know we got seventeen dollars and thirteen cents left, but things is terrible dear.''

"But I'm so hot. Really. I feel like a baked apple. You can stay here if you like and I'll go and get it. Give me some money.''

Reluctantly Susan gave Rose twenty-five cents.

Out on the platform, Rose found a lemonade stall and asked for two cups. She discovered that there was only the one tin cup attached by a string to the stand, so she had her drink and hurried back to Susan.

"You have to go, he doesn't have any cups.''

"How much?''

"It's only five cents.''

"Five cents? A whole five cents for one cup of lemonade? I don't want none.''

"Don't be silly, Susan. It's good.''

"I don't want none. Five cents! The man who sold it to you is a thief.''

"That's right, girlie, you tell 'em.'' The drunk in the seat behind leaned forward breathing whisky in their faces. "You got brains in that pretty little head of yours. I like that.''

Susan shrank away from him and said nothing. Rose glared at him over the back of the seat. He frowned at her, leaned forward and pulled her nose. "Mind your manners, sonny,'' he growled. "You better sit back here and let me sit with the little lady so her and me can talk.'' He staggered to his feet.

Stunned by the surprise of the attack on her nose and the sudden pain, Rose just stared at the man. But before he could make another move, Mrs. Heilbrunner leaned across the aisle and said sharply, "Don't you pester those youngsters!'

At that moment, the conductor came through and the drunk sat back in his own seat, grumbling and muttering about meddlesome old hens.

The bell clanged, the whistle blew, the conductor shouted his "All aboard!" and the train started.

"Did he hurt you?" Susan whispered.

"No," said Rose, but he had, and he had frightened her. She was relieved when she heard him begin to snore loudly. Susan dozed beside her.

They were travelling east across the state through the Mohawk Valley. The landscape looked more and more desolate with every click of the train's wheels. "It's them seventeen-year locusts," Mrs. Heilbrunner told her. "My ma says them bugs has ate up everything in Upper New York State that grows, and lots that don't." The grain had been neatly stacked near Oswego and across the lake in Canada. Here everything was chewed to the ground. In the August heat, with the coal dust along the train tracks, it was a dismal sight.

"My ma says she don't know how they're going to feed us all because of them locusts." Mrs. Heilbrunner sighed. "But she says she's supposing the Lord will provide and I'm supposing that too. What else can we do?"

Rose listened to bits of conversation from other passengers talking in voices loud enough to sound over the squalling of Mrs. Heilbrunner's children and the clickety-click of the train wheels. Someone was singing "The Union Forever" in an off-key baritone and the man in the seat behind woke now and then to curse mumblingly into his beard.

Rose was so hungry she had a headache, and the day was sweltering. There was no breeze. To open the window meant coal dust and large cinders flying in. Coal dust lay over everything — it was even in her teeth.

They reached Albany in the late afternoon. Rose climbed up and brought down the suitcase. She said goodbye to Mrs. Heilbrunner who wished them a tearful Godspeed, then with Susan clinging to her hand, she led the way into the station. Susan, so calm and capable at home, was unexpectedly terrified in the pushing, shouting city throngs. She had never in her life seen such crowds. Her nervousness worried Rose, and she no longer felt that euphoria that had set them both giggling wildly the evening before. The station was jammed with people. Men with megaphones were shouting the arrival of their train and three others on their way to New York, Boston and Montreal. A group of soldiers was being greeted with cheers and a band playing "When Johnny Comes Marching Home", and everywhere the hawkers shouted their wares. By pushing and shoving, and hitting people with the edge of the suitcase, Rose got them through the crowd, found their train and got them on it. Susan was white. Her jaw was set.

"There's so many people, Rose!"

Rose was about to reply that there were a lot more people in New York City when she was interrupted by a familiar, rasping voice.

"All right, now, boy, you just move away and let the little lady and me have a nice talk." A hand grabbed the collar of her shirt and she was lifted out into the aisle. It was the drunk from the seat behind them in the Syracuse train. He reached past her and took Susan by the arm. There was a nasty smile on his face.

"Rose," gasped Susan. Without stopping to think, Rose grabbed Susan's arm and yanked. The drunk was so surprised he let go of her other arm, and Rose fled with her from the car.

They ran down the platform, through the station and out onto the street beyond. There they crouched down behind a carriage that stood waiting to pick up passengers coming from the train.

After a few minutes, Rose had caught her breath. "We have to go back, Susan. Our stuff's in the train." She stood up resolutely. Susan was shaking so hard her teeth were chattering. "I can't," she whispered, "I can't. I'm afraid of that man."

"Then you stay here." But Susan would not stay alone so they went back into the station together. Rose had completely lost her bearings in their flight and had to ask directions all over again for the train to New York.

"Better hurry, son." The man at the information desk looked up at the clock. "I'm not sure that train's still here."

They started to run, bumping into people, tripping over baggage, frantically making their way around vendors' stalls, and reached the platform just in time to see the last car pull away from the station.

Susan started to cry. Rose swallowed her own threatening tears and thought furiously.

"It's all right, Susan. The suitcase will go to New York and we can get it at the 'lost and found'. I've done that with my grandmother. We still have our tickets so we can stay here until the next train comes. Even if it doesn't come until tomorrow. We can wait."

"We can't," wailed Susan, "the tickets and our money are on the seat of the train. We don't got nothing at all!"

ALONG THE RIVER

"Don't be silly, Susan, you must have the money. How are we going to get to New York without the tickets or the money?"

"I don't know," Susan whispered. The frightened expression in her big black eyes made her look like a dog that expected to be hit. Rose wanted to hit her. She stamped across the platform and into the station in a high rage, a rage that, although she did not realize it, was masking her own terrible fear of being lost, stranded in a time and place she did not know. She had to lash out at Susan to give herself strength.

"How could she have?" she muttered angrily. "How could she have been so stupid? Well, she'll just have to figure out a way to get us there, that's all. I'm not going to." She pushed her hot sticky hair back from her angry face and jammed her hands into her pockets — and realized that she had money. She pulled it out, the twenty cents change from the lemonade at Syracuse. She went straight to the buffet and bought a meat pie, an ice cream and a glass of lemonade. Greedily and speedily she ate it all. She found a washroom but it cost a penny so she left, muttering crossly to herself, "I suppose they expect you to wet yourself." All the same the food had made her feel better and she went looking for Susan.

She found her out on the platform, huddled in a corner behind a baggage cart. Her face was red and streaked with grime and tears, and her bonnet had slipped to one side. At the sight of her, Rose felt a twinge of remorse. The ice cream and the meat pie flip-flopped uneasily in her stomach. She found she did not want to look Susan in the eye, neither could she tell her what she had done. Putting her hand guiltily to her mouth to feel if there were crumbs, she swallowed to cover her nervousness.

"Now ,then." She cleared her throat. "What we have to do is figure out what to do next. Do you have any ideas?"

Susan looked at her blankly.

"You know, for getting to New York."

"We got nothing but our own two feet, Rose. I don't see we got much choice."

"No." Rose's bluster wilted. "I guess not." She hitched herself up onto the baggage cart and looked down at her coal black hands, wriggling her toes in her running shoes. Albany? Where was Albany? And how were they going to get to Washington from Albany with no money? She closed her eyes and recited mechanically: "Albany is the capital of New York. It's a hundred and forty-five miles from New York City and it's on the Hudson River." Once again she was grateful for her grandmother's lessons. "So I suppose what we have to do now is find the river, and follow it to New York." She brightened for a moment. "When we get there everything will be O.K. because I know New York. A hundred and forty-five miles isn't so far, is it? I bet we've come that far already today.''

''Yes, but we was in the train and now all we got is our feet and no place to sleep for the night and nothing to eat.''

At the word eat, Rose winced. ''We'll manage,'' she said quickly, ''we'll manage. Maybe we can just stop somewhere and ask for some supper and the people will let us sleep in their house.''

''Rose! I ain't no beggar. We've got to start up like you say and hope by tomorrow morning there's going to be folks who'll let us work for 'em so's we can get breakfast and maybe earn a bit to get us going. We just got to pray we don't run into no one with no nasty notions.'' She shuddered.

''I suppose so.'' Rose grimaced. She didn't like the idea of working for somebody. The picture Susan brought to mind was of having to live for weeks or months in an attic, like poor Sara Crewe with only crusts of bread to eat and stale water to drink, and she didn't like it even though it was romantic to read about. She wished fleetingly that she was back at Hawthorn Bay, and sighed. ''I guess we might as well find the river.'' She hopped down from the baggage cart and went into the station building once more.

By this time the band, the soldiers and their families had left, the crowds had thinned, and some of the vendors were shutting up their stands. Rose asked the man at the information desk how to get to the river. He guffawed loudly and said ''Why you just use your two feet, sonny, just use your two feet,'' and pointed east.

They left the building and looked east and there

below them, not two hundred yards away, was the Hudson River glinting in the afternoon sun, the blue hills of the Catskills in the distance.

"This way to New York," said Rose. They started down the hill past shacks with little gardens of cabbages, tomatoes, and beans, thickly covered with coal soot ("I wouldn't want to eat none of them," whispered Susan as they hurried past), and came, at last, to the deep mud flats, the docks, the warehouses, and the river, wide and green, flowing deeply, steadily towards New York City.

They walked until they had put the busy docks and warehouses of Albany behind them. They sat down to rest on a small deserted fishing wharf and watched the gulls and sandpipers, and listened to the steady lap, lap of the water against the wooden pilings. Susan took off her bonnet, leaned over the edge of the wharf and with her cupped hands brought water to her face to wash. She dried her hands on the cattails that grew at the edge of the river. She was still streaked with black but she looked brighter. Wordlessly, Rose followed suit.

"Why don't we take off our things and get in?" she suggested.

"Rose!" Susan was scandalized. "Just because we got no money don't mean we ain't still decent folks. Look at all those men out in the boats."

Out on the river, barges and fishing boats were headed towards shore, the men shouting goodnatured banter at one another as they prepared to come in for the night.

"I think we'd better get on," Susan said, uneasy.

"All right." Wearily Rose got to her feet. The tide was low and the muddy shore was full of shells, dead fish, and horseshoe crabs, as well as bottles and old boards, so they walked well back, along the fringe of river weeds and tough grass. Now and then a fisherman on his way home said, "Good evening." Sometimes a dog barked, a cow mooed. Voices in the distance called to one another as the day settled into evening. The hills grew dark, looming over them like giants huddled in black cloaks, watchful, mysterious.

The mud gave way to a different shoreline, sandier, and along the high-tide line there were trees, poplars, dogwoods and occasionally bare sandy patches. Cautiously they picked their way through the dusk. Every time they heard a small animal rustling in the grass, or a startled bird flutter in the trees, they started and then, more cautiously than before, moved on.

"We got to stop soon." Susan's voice sounded exhausted. They halted by a large tree.

"Maybe we can find a barn or something. I don't like it right outside like this."

"Ain't nothing out here going to hurt us near as bad as what might get us if we start hanging around in somebody's barn." Susan made a move to start up again. Suddenly, she stopped. "Rose! What's that?"

There was the sound of someone thrashing around not more than three feet from them. They froze.

Rustle, rustle, stomp, stomp, the sound of heavy breathing. Susan began to laugh shakily.

"Soo boss," she said softly, "soo boss." In answer there was a long, drawn out, "mooooo."

They walked around the tree and there, its white patches glimmering in the twilight, was a large black and white cow.

"Soo, bossy, soo." Susan stroked it gently between its eyes and behind its ears. It nuzzled happily against her.

"We could stay here with the cow," said Rose, hopefully. "We could have some of its milk. You can milk a cow."

"That'd be stealing. This here's someone's back pasture. We ain't staying here."

Away from the crowds, back in the countryside, Susan was again her own capable self. Nothing Rose could say would persuade her to change her mind, so they proceeded in glum silence.

They had been pushing their way through dark bushes for almost half an hour when they smelled cooking.

"Chicken," said Susan.

"Doesn't that smell wonderful!" Rose sighed.

"Don't pay no mind. We got to steer clear. We don't know who it is."

Susan put her hand nervously on Rose's arm. They crept slowly, step by step, along the shore. They were edging their way around a thick clump of bushes when they almost fell into a small clearing where a chicken, spitted on a stick, was cooking over a low fire. There was nobody in sight.

"Doesn't it smell good?" breathed Rose.

"Don't you set one foot near that there bird! The Lord knows who's cooking it or what he might do if he was to catch us here. Let's get going."

There was a rustle in the bushes behind them. "Hands up or I'll spit you on this knife and add you to my dinner," growled a harsh voice.

Rose felt the hair on the back of her neck stand

straight out and her heart lurched in terror. Susan gasped and leaped aside. They both raised their hands.

"Now you just move along so's I can see what I got here."

Something sharp pricked Rose in the shoulder. Terrified, she stumbled into the clearing, half shoving Susan before her.

"Kids," said the voice contemptuously. "You alone?" he asked suspiciously.

They nodded.

"Where you from?"

They were both too afraid to speak.

"I ain't gonna hurt you," said the soldier, for the man who came around to stand before them was dressed in the faded blue uniform of the Union army. He was grey haired, small, and thin as a coat hanger, with a face that was worn into two lines on either cheek, so deep they were clearly visible through his untidy grey beard. He had only one arm.

"I ain't gonna hurt you," he repeated in an aggrieved tone, "and what's more I expect I'm gonna have to share my dinner with you. You hungry?"

Rose had almost recovered from her fright. The roasting chicken which the soldier leaned down to turn smelled like a banquet. She nodded. "We're very hungry."

"I suppose you might as well set," the soldier said glumly. "I didn't mean to give you such a scare" — his tone softened — "but you see I'm like you — I suppose you're waifs with no money and no place to go. I lost all my money to a card shark down to Washington. I'm on my way home to Hoosick Falls but there ain't nobody'll give work to a one-arm soldier — or a soldier of any kind for that matter," he added bitterly. "We was just fine and wonderful and it seemed the whole United States was dying to weep over us and sing out 'Glory Halleluiah' and 'Johnny Come Marching Home' — until we started to come home. Then, bang, the doors was shut against us. Seems the whole world is afraid of us. I warrant folks are even afraid of the little drummer boys, nine, ten years old. Killers, they say. Trained killers. You'd think we all been having fun. Gettysburg. Chancellorsville. Cold Harbor. I was at all them swell places. And while I was having me such a good time my wife took off with another fella. 'I'm afraid I have to make other arrangements, Joe,' she said, 'because there isn't no money comin' in.' Of course there wasn't no money. The blessed government wasn't givin' us none for all that fun we was having, not regular they wasn't. But we stuck with old Abe, God rest his soul. And now there ain't nobody wants us." His rough, angry voice ceased abruptly and he poked the fire with a stick.

"You got a lot of trouble, mister," said Susan.

"Yeah, yeah," he said crossly. "What about you kids? What brings you to the river late at night like this?"

Rose told him that they were brother and sister on their way to Washington to find their older brother. She told him about the man on the train and losing their money.

"But we're going to get it back in New York City," she said.

"I wouldn't make no plans to that effect," said the soldier dryly. "What's more I wouldn't hang on too hard to that notion of findin' your brother. They're moving soldiers out of them hospitals as fast as they can move 'em. I know. I was in one of them places for this," he shrugged his armless shoulder. Susan paled. Rose, somewhat shamefacedly, turned her eyes away from the empty, pinned-up sleeve.

"If that brother of yours is still alive, chances are he's on his way home and you're gonna miss him. You might better turn yourselves right straight around and wait for him back there."

The soldier told them his name was Joe Haggerty, and he said he didn't know Will though he had been in battle with the 81st regiment. By that time the chicken was ready. Joe cut it up with the knife that had been so murderous only a little while earlier, put the pieces on his tin plate and passed them around.

"I never stole nothin before I went in the army," Joe Haggerty said mournfully around bites of chicken. "We soon found out if we was gonna get dinner to fight on we was gonna have to help ourselves, and now I don't mind a bit. If folks isn't gonna share out the work, they're just gonna have to share out the dinner anyways. Yessir, the miserable cussed, mean-minded, penny-pinchin. . . ." He spat out a bone with such force that it thunked against a tree.

Joe continued to call down God's curses on the populace, the army, the hospitals, and his wife in particular, until finally he grew tired, retreated from them to make ready for the night and settled down near the fire, his coat flung over him. The girls followed his example, huddling close together for warmth.

The next morning, before the sun was up, they had left the riverside and followed Joe a half mile up the hill to the highway.

"You won't find no work nor food following the river," he told them. "You got to follow the road. Goes to the same place, New York City. If you'd take my advice you'd get on home. Like I said, you ain't gonna find your brother in Washington, not alive, you ain't." And with that last dismal warning, he gave a half-hearted wave with his good arm and turned north.

Rose looked at Susan. Susan looked at Rose.

"It ain't so," said Susan firmly, and Rose, responding to her assurance, took a deep breath and said, "So what we have to do now, is just go."

"You always say that," Susan laughed, and in that comradely frame of mind they set off on the road to New York.

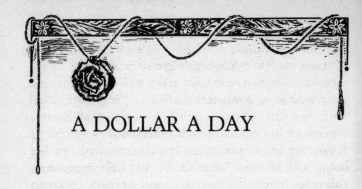

A DOLLAR A DAY

At the first farmhouse they came to, while Rose waited
on the road, Susan went around to the back door and
knocked. She was back in a minute. "She ain't got
work," she said.

At the next farm, it was the same, and at the next.
"They mostly got kids as big as us who can do all they
need done," said Susan.

"They shouldn't have so many kids," grumbled
Rose. "I'm starved. My stomach hurts."

They had been walking for almost an hour, when they
reached a small village, its blacksmith, general store,
church and houses centred around a green. They got
themselves a drink from the well that stood on the
green, and sat down on a bench opposite a bakeshop. It
was still early and the shopkeepers were just opening up
for the day, shaking out carpets, sweeping their steps,
setting out their wares. They watched the baker put
buns and cakes in his window.

"Rose." Susan's face brightened. "Rose, you got
money. Remember? Yesterday when you went and got
lemonade and I didn't have none. You got twenty cents.
Look in your pocket."

Rose's stomach tightened. Her face grew hot. "I lost it," she said quickly.

"Look in your pockets. It's got to be there."

"It isn't. I lost it. I forgot to tell you. I . . . Susan, why are you looking at me like that?"

"I ain't sure."

Rose got up from the bench and took a few steps across the grass. She could feel Susan's eyes on her back. "Oh, all right," she said crossly, whirling around, "all right. I spent it. I spent it on something to eat when I was mad at you because you left the tickets and the money on the train."

Susan stared at her in disbelief. Tears came to her eyes. She stood up and without a word started towards the road, her head high, her back stiff.

"Susan, wait!" Rose came up beside her.

"I don't want to walk with you." Susan kept a brisk pace along the road that led out of the village.

Rose fell back. She felt hated, the way she had felt the time she had overheard Sam tell his mother how ugly and disagreeable she was. And this time she knew she deserved it. She felt worse than she had after Aunt Nan's accident. She was ashamed, she was willing to do any kind of work, ask anybody for anything if only Susan wouldn't walk ahead like that — so fast, so stiff and straight, so cold. "I've never had a friend before," she thought, and she was suddenly very much afraid of losing Susan's friendship. She sat down on a fallen tree and let Susan get well out of sight before she started up again.

At the first house outside the village she stopped. An old man came to the door.

"Have you got any jobs?" she asked nervously.

"You're the second kid come along this way in ten minutes looking for work," said the old man sourly and closed the door in her face.

Humiliated, she gritted her teeth and marched down the road. "I don't suppose it's much good us coming one after the other to the same house." The next house was big and handsome, with white pillars around a curved porch in front, its lawns closely cropped and decorated with bright flowerbeds. As Rose reached it, a man galloped up on a horse.

"You, boy, how would you like to earn five cents?" he shouted as he leaped off at the front door.

When she ran up, nodding vigorously, he handed her the reins of his horse. "He's gentle but he needs to be held firmly," said the man and ran up the wide curved steps of the house.

The horse, a big dapple grey, was gentle but wilful and he wanted to eat the asters and marigolds that grew along the walk. Rose spent a back-breaking half hour tugging on his reins, round the drive, along the road and back, until her hand was blistered and her temper was sore.

"Will and Susan can both drown in the Atlantic ocean! And I hate you whatever your name is," she whispered passionately in his ear, and tugged furiously at his reins to vent her feelings.

He gave a startled whinny and looked around at her. She was sure he was laughing. She grabbed the reins more tightly, but before she could give him the shake she intended, the man came out of the house.

Seeing her grim, red face and the horse craning his neck towards the flowers again, the man laughed heartily. He was a tall, thin man with a thin nondescript face, but when he laughed he whooped and bellowed and cackled with such pleasure that he became quite astonishing to watch and Rose could not help laughing too.

"He's got the soul of a goat, that Hermes," he said, "the soul of a goat. You're fortunate he didn't eat your shirt — eat your shirt, upon my word, you're fortunate. You're a good lad." He gave her ten cents and, with one quick leap, mounted his horse.

"Thank you," said Rose weakly. "Thank you very much."

The man looked down at her in surprise.

"You don't come from around here," he said.

"I come from Canada."

"You're a long way from home, little Canuck, God bless." And off he rode.

Rose clutched the precious ten-cent piece in the hand that wasn't blistered and raced down the road to find Susan.

"What if I can't find her?" she whispered as she ran. "What if she's working in some house? What if she decided to go home?"

"Rose." Susan was sitting on a rail fence that edged a field beside the road.

Rose stopped. She walked over and held out the ten cents. "I owe you ten more," she said awkwardly.

Susan didn't take the money. "It ain't so much the money, Rose. It's just I didn't know you was mean."

Rose flushed from her toes to her scalp. She didn't say anything. A squirrel scampered up a nearby chestnut tree, chattering.

"Come on," said Susan shortly, climbing down from the fence, "we got to get us something to eat."

Rose shook her head. "It's your money, I don't want anything."

"Who's going to carry you when you're so hungry you faint?"

"You can leave me."

"Rose, we got troubles enough without you should start feeling sorry for yourself. Now pick up and come on."

Feeling both hated and hateful, Rose followed Susan down the road. At the next farmhouse they came to, their ten cents bought them a lot more than ten cents had bought at the railroad station in Albany. They ate eggs and bread and butter and drank a glass of milk each. The woman watched them suspiciously while they ate and told them they could wash at her well for another ten cents.

"No, thank you, ma'am," said Susan.

Past farms and meadows, across streams, through three small villages they tramped and there was no work. They did not speak. Susan kept up a steady pace until Rose was so tired and footsore, so totally wretched, that she sat down at the side of the road and watched, without feeling, as a large green and black garter snake slithered away through the grass with a frog in its mouth. She put her head down on her knees and closed her eyes. After a time she felt Susan come and sit down beside her.

"It's an awful hot place t'sit."

"I don't care."

They said nothing more for a few minutes. It was past

noon. The sun blazed down on them through a grey haze. Few birds sang in the noon heat. Only the cicadas with their fretful buzzing brought any sign of life to the wilting landscape. Traffic on the road was desultory — now and then a buggy rattled by or a farmer's wagon. Sometimes a horseman clop-clopped along. In the distance the train whistle tooted.

"We got to get going," said Susan, rising to her feet. "The last milepost said we come sixteen mile from Albany and if your calculation is right we got a long ways to go."

Rose pushed her hands through her dusty, dirty hair which was by this time a dull brown colour and sticking out all over her head. She looked sideways at Susan.

"I'm sorry about the money," she said.

"I expect you are," said Susan and that, Rose felt sure, was all the word she was going to get out of Susan on that subject.

That afternoon they were lucky. They came to the village of Paiseley around five o'clock. It was a village very like the others they had passed through, with a cluster of houses and stores around a green on which stood the village well and a small bandstand. In addition, stretched out across the green, was a long table made up of several tables end to end, with places set for all the people in the village.

A band was tuning up in the bandstand, the green was full of people — women setting the table with all kinds of pickles and relishes, platters of cold chicken and beef, salads, and fruits; small children running around, shouting, or being shouted orders by their mothers — "Here, you, Johnny, you take this paper and swat them flies!'' ''Alice, you run across t'Misses VanArpen 'n tell her we're a mite short on butter!'' And the men — young and old, soldiers in uniform — were gathered on the green in knots, talking and laughing. There was a great feeling of joy and excitement which did as much to pick up the girls' tired spirits as did the sight of all the food.

''Can we help?'' Susan asked an old man, who was sitting at the edge of the village green, and seemed to be organizing the celebrations, waving his stick and rattling off directions.

''You passing through? Where're you from? Where're you headed, girl?''

Susan told him about Will. The old man looked at them both intently. ''Wait here,'' he said and standing up carefully, went into a nearby house. He came back with a square of blue and white checked cloth in his hand. He went along the full length of the table putting meat and cheese and buns and cakes into the square of cloth. ''The vegetables is kind of skinny on account of them locusts,'' he said. Then he slowly and methodically tied the four corners of the cloth together and handed it to Rose.

''Here, young feller, you carry this, and never let anyone say that James Campbell ain't a thankful man nor that the village of Paiseley don't know how to celebrate. We're celebrating the return of our boys, and may the good Lord bring your soldier home safe as he brung' mine.'' He thrust the bundle of food into Rose's hand and turned back to fussing over how the preparations were coming along.

''Thanks, mister,'' said Susan, ''God bless you.''

The little scene had gathered a small audience which so embarrassed Rose that she forgot to say thank you.

Rose was all for sitting down beside the road and eating the food right there but Susan said, "No, this ain't the place to stop." Almost a mile and a half later they came to a little wood where they found a stream and there Susan stopped. Gratefully they took off their shoes and stockings, and they sat with their feet in the stream while they ate their way through all but two pieces of cheese and two buns. "We got to save them for breakfast," said Susan. Reluctantly Rose agreed and they settled into a silence which, although not as companionable as it might have been, was easier than anything they had achieved since morning.

They travelled the road for over a week, managing ten or twelve miles a day. Though the fields were dry and chewed up and sad, the distant hills were green and blue and glinting in the sunlight. Sometimes they passed through woods and surprised deer or raccoons, squirrels and chipmunks. The birds sang noisily. They always made Rose think of Will. Now and then the road dipped down into a valley to pursue its path almost by the river's edge and then the steady lapping of the water as its tides rose and fell was a kind of song to march to. Rose felt secure by the river. She knew she couldn't get lost. The river would take her to New York.

It rained once or twice, but mostly they were dry, scorching days that burned their skin and blistered Rose's feet. They slept in woods or fields, and washed in the river, in brooks and tiny streams. One night they sheltered from a thunderstorm in an old fishing shack by the river, huddled together against the bursts of white light that illuminated then obscured the black hills.

Sometimes they were lucky and found work and ate well. Other times they went to sleep hungry. They hoed gardens, washed windows, ran errands to earn twenty-five or fifty cents. Once they white-washed a hen house for a dollar. More than once they held horses for pennies. Sometimes they got rides with kind farmers but the rides were slow. Once they rode in a buggy with a pair of travelling players.

While their clothes grew thinner and dirtier and their shoes were dangerously worn, their bodies grew tough and sunburned. They learned to ask for work and to take abuse from strangers. Once Rose was chased by a gang of boys in a village who shouted and swore at her and threw ripe tomatoes. Once an old woman called them "thieving children" and threatened them with the county jail. Another time, passing through a town on a Saturday evening, Susan was bothered by a man who sidled up to her and offered to buy her a pretty dress if she would show him a good time. Rose was not taken unawares as she had been on the train in Albany. She came up behind him, poked her finger in his back and threatened to shoot.

"I'm just out of the army," she growled. "The toughest drummer boy in the 81st regiment."

"O.K., kid. Didn't mean nothing by it." The man had slunk away.

"What made you think to say that?" Susan was full of relief and admiration.

"I remembered what Joe Haggerty said: 'They're all afraid of soldiers.' And see, they are, even little ones."

For the first time since Susan had found out about

Rose spending the money, they had a real laugh together. They had patched over the trouble between them by not mentioning it but it had not gone away. It was like a bandaged sore. Rose was aware every day that Susan did not feel the same way about her as she had on that morning that seemed so long ago when they had set out from Hawthorn Bay. She was polite, kind, and thoughtful, because that was what Susan was, but the companionship they had felt was missing. It was almost as though they had a job to do together (although they never mentioned that either) and, when that job was done, they would say goodbye to each other like two strangers.

One morning they washed in a small stream. Rose looked disgustedly at the remnants of her socks, two lengths of grey, tattered cloth. She stuffed them into the knot-hole of a tree.

"Even the robins won't want to make nests out of them," said Susan. "They can have my bonnet. It's got almost as many holes as a sieve." She tied the misshapen black straw to a branch. She looked ruefully down at her dress, by now grimy and thin. "Ain't nothing much to be done about that."

Rose's jeans had holes in both knees and were crusty with dirt. She was so used to them she hardly noticed.

"Come on," she said. "We *must* keep going."

As the sun came up over the hills, they reached the edge of a small village whose signpost announced that it was called Dorland. Opposite was a little unpainted store in front of which stood a blacksmith shop. The shop was quiet and the smith was standing outside, his hands on his hips, looking very disgruntled.

"You, boy," he called, when he caught sight of them

coming along the road, "you want a job?" He was a squat, swarthy man with hairy arms and straight black hair, and a beard that almost hid his small tight mouth.

Rose crossed the road to stand beside him. "How much money?" she asked boldly.

He looked her up and down. "You're pretty small," he said. "Give you twenty-five cents a day and room and board."

Rose went back to where Susan waited. "Twenty-five cents a day isn't very much," she whispered. "We'd only have a dollar and seventy-five cents at the end of a whole week. I'm not going to do it." Susan nodded.

"No thank you," she called. They started on their way.

"Wait! Come here, boy. I can see you're a bright little lad. Now if you was to work hard for me I might see my way clear to give you a whole dollar."

Rose looked at Susan. Susan said in a low voice, "If I could find work in th'village and earn the same, at the end of the week we'd have fourteen dollars and we could get back on the train all the way to Washington. I think you might better tell the man yes."

"I'll do it," said Rose and, with those words, began the most miserable week she had ever spent in her life. While Susan went off up the road to look for work, Rose was led into the darkness of the blacksmith's shop.

Her chief job was to wield the bellows so that the fire in the forge would burn hot enough for the smith to soften his horseshoes, wagon wheels and plough points over it. The forge looked to Rose like a big, brick barbeque without a grill on top and with a hole in the side, just under the fire box, for the bellows to blow air through. The bellows was like a huge fan made of accordion folds of leather, attached at one end to the floor, with a large handle at the other end which the bellows boy was to pump vigorously up and down to drive the air that kept the fire roaring.

The shop was deep and close. Its only light came from the one door at the front and the red glowing fire. The two windows at either side were permanently shut and covered with black dust. It was only after her eyes had become used to the dark that Rose could see what else was there besides the forge, the bellows, and the anvil on which the smith pounded the white hot metal into shape — the ringing of metal on metal deafening to the ears and the flying sparks frightening to watch. There were kegs towards the back, full of horseshoes and nails and spare bits of farm machinery. There were rings along one side wall for horses to be tied to while they were being shod. There was a bucket full of cold water which Rose was required to cart from the well that stood just off to the east of the shop. The water was for quenching the hot metal when the smith was finished shaping it and its sizzle and steam made the whole shop seem to Rose like descriptions she had read in books of torture chambers and dungeons.

Nor was the smith a friendly man. He said nothing all morning except to let loose a long stream of curses if something went wrong. He stopped once at midday and brought out a lunch of bread, lard and cheese, of which he gave Rose a very small portion. He had a bottle of beer for himself. Rose had water from the well. The only thing he said to her as he was getting up from his lunch was, ''Too hot to work. Farmers be in all afternoon with

their horses." And they were, from early afternoon until
the shadows grew long. They stood around outside and
looked curiously at Rose but no one spoke to her, while
Peter Maas (Rose learned that that was his name by
listening to the men) poked the horseshoes into the
glowing coals with his long tongs and she pumped furiously at the bellows, feeling sure, at first, that her arms
would fall off, and then growing so numb she hardly
cared.

When evening came at last, Peter Maas put down his
hammers and left the forge.

"Stay by until the fire dies," he growled and stumped
off up the lane to his shack. Rose didn't know what to
do. She was very hungry and so tired she was almost
falling over. She waited by the fire. Peter Maas did not
come back. She heard voices from the village but no one
came near the blacksmith shop. There was no sign of
Susan. The fire died down. She fell asleep, her back
against the front of the shop.

When she woke, the sun was coming up over the distant hills. She got up, drank at the well and splashed
water on her face. She stretched her tired legs and
almost cried with the stiff pain in her arms. She was
dizzy with hunger.

"A dollar a day will take us to New York," she told
herself grimly and that refrain kept her going for the rest
of the terrible week. Peter Maas came down from his
house early that first morning.

"Here, boy," he said (he never asked her name nor
told her his), and gave her another slice of the thick
brown bread with lard on it. He started work at once and
stopped only for his brief lunch. That night he told

Rose, "There's a bed in behind the shop" and left her another slice of bread and lard. She slept on a narrow iron cot and sometimes dreamed of Sam or Aunt Nan or Grandmother, too tired to care where she was. "A dollar a day will take us to New York," she would murmur and fall asleep. "A dollar a day will take us to New York," she would tell herself as she was getting up. "A dollar a day will take us to New York," she would chant to the rhythm of the bellows and the hammer on the anvil. The fourth evening Susan came. She was horrified to see Rose almost exhausted and covered with such black soot she looked as though she had been painted with stove black. She had had a chance to wash not only herself but her clothes and looked fresh and bright.

"Oh, Rose!" Susan was aghast. "You oughtn't to be doing this."

"A dollar a day will get us to New York," said Rose tiredly. "How are you, Susan?"

"I ain't so bad. I got work helping out where a hired girl's took sick. I get fifty cents a day plus room and board. Is he feeding you good?"

Rose told Susan about the bread and lard. The next evening Susan came running up the road with a bundle under her arm. "I ain't supposed to be out," she whispered and ran off.

The bundle had in it some cheese, a tomato, a bit of cold beef and a small jar of milk. Rose stared at the feast in disbelief. Then she gobbled it all up, stuffing food into her mouth like a ravening dog.

Susan did not come again and Rose figured that she must have been in trouble for bringing the food. She ate bread and lard and the bit of noontime cheese, with the grateful memory of Susan's meal until the end of the week.

At the end of the week, when it came evening, Rose put down the bellows. "I've been here a week, Mr. Maas," she said, "and I'm going to leave now. You owe me seven dollars."

It took all the courage she had to stand up to that dour, bad-tempered man and ask for her money. The only reason she could do it was because the refrain "A dollar a day will take us to New York" had become so firmly lodged in her brain that it sang itself even while she was asking for her pay.

"Seven dollars!" Peter Maas gave a short laugh that sounded more like a terrier's bark than a man's laugh. "Seven dollars! Boy, I pay twenty-five cents a day. That's what I told you when you come."

Rose turned cold with anger. "You said if I worked hard you'd give me a dollar a day."

"As I recall . . . ." Peter drew the words out slowly, his face lighting with the only humour Rose had seen in him all week. "As I recall, I said if you worked real hard I might see my way clear to giving you a dollar. I didn't say a dollar a day." He chuckled, pulled a small roll of bills out of his pocket and slowly took one off the top.

Rage blew up in Rose like a Roman candle, straight up and bursting with heat and speed. With no thought in her head but how she hated that ugly smile, she reached out and snatched the roll of bills from his hand and ran.

She heard horses' hooves behind her but she didn't stop. She heard Peter Maas bellow, "Thief! Thief! Stop him!" She heard shouts and the sound of feet pounding after her on the road. She ran, her lungs nearly bursting, her legs pumping furiously; straight through the village she ran, down a side road, up a farmer's lane, over a bridge, off up a slope and down the other side, where she stopped. Spent, she clung, like a burr to a blanket, to the side of the slope, a hunted animal gasping with long shuddering breaths. She heard the feet pounding after her, the sound hollow over the little bridge, then, miraculously, she heard them continue on along the lane.

Her breath gradually slowed down. The sound of feet came back — and boys' voices, loud and laughing, followed by the sound of horses' hooves.

"Wouldn't I give a good kick to have seen old Maas's face when that feller stole his money!" said one.

"I just wish I had a share of it," said another. "Only feller in the history of Dorland to get anything out of old Maas."

Their voices faded as they disappeared in the direction of the village.

After a time, Rose peered out from behind her slope and there, standing perfectly still, was a horse and rider. She jumped back, looking frantically for a place to run to.

Before she could gather herself for flight, she heard a familiar voice say, "Upon my word, I believe it's the little Canadian boy under all that pitch."

Rose came out from behind the hill. The large dapple-grey horse was happily munching the leaves of a wild apple tree that grew beside the lane.

"Hello, Hermes," she said. The horse looked up, whinnied and went back to his meal.

"You're a fine lad," said the man, "a fine lad. I knew

it the second I laid eyes on you. By Jove, yes I did." And
he began to laugh that amazing laugh that Rose remembered from their brief encounter outside Albany. Chort-
ling, cackling, bellowing, hooting, absurd laughter that
no one listening to could keep from laughing back at.
So, rubbing black soot from the corner of one eye,
aching and sore, Rose laughed back.

"Heard the whole exchange, upon my word, heard it
all," said the man. "Splendid boy, how much did you
lift?" And off he went into gales and whoops of laughter,
slapping his thigh and rocking in his saddle — and all
the while Hermes, unconcerned, ate away at the apple
tree.

Rose looked down at the crumpled money she still
had clutched in her hand. She smoothed out the bills
and counted them — eleven one-dollar bills.

"He only owed me seven," she said.

"Don't give it a thought," said the man, "not the
smallest particle of a thought. Quite obviously the man
is a skinflint, a welsher who doesn't pay up what he
owes. Therefore it was right and proper for you to take
what was yours. And, if you got a dollar or two more
into the bargain, why so much the better for you." And
off he went again into peals of laughter.

"Plucky little fellow," he said at last, "plucky little
fellow, now what do you propose to do? Wouldn't go
back to that village just now, be a foolish move, very
foolish move. Get on with the excursion if I were you."

"Excursion?"

"Indeed. The pilgrimage, the march you're engaged
on, the mission you've undertaken. Whatever it was
that took you from your frozen northland and brought
you to our fair lands."

"I can't," she said. "My sister's back there."

"Well, my young friend, I don't know how long it's been since I've had such amusement, I've half a mind to hire you to keep me entertained but since I don't imagine for a moment that you'd agree to it, and furthermore I travel too much to accommodate you, I'll polish off the evening in fine style for us both, in gratitude for the diversion. I'll find your sister and buy you a dinner into the bargain. All you have to do is fold up your fortune and put it safely away in your pocket — I suppose you have a pocket somewhere under that tar — and I shall take care of the rest."

Bemused, Rose sat down beside the hill and waited, rejoicing in her good luck and at the same time not quite trusting it. How was the man going to find Susan? He had gone off without ever asking what she looked like. But, not twenty minutes later, she heard the beat of a horse's hooves and then Hermes appeared with two figures on his back. Susan had a large bundle.

The man leaped down from his horse and handed Susan down with the grace of an old-time courtier. Before either Rose or Susan had a chance to speak, he bowed to them each in turn and said, "There you are, my young friends, delivered out of the lions' den. As I have far to go, and old Hermes cannot manage three human beings, however small the third, and as you are no doubt accustomed to the ways of the road, please accept this cash for the meal I promised, then I must be off. I wish, I truly wish I could avail myself of your company a while longer as I suspect your tale is an interesting one — brother and sister you most assuredly are not — but alas, I have no time." With a flourish, he handed Rose a five-dollar bill. "Now dine in style, my young friends," he said, "dine in style. Augustus Delfinney at your service."

Doffing his hat, Augustus Delfinney rode back up the lane towards the village and into the darkening hills.

"Susan, did you ever see anyone like that man in all your life?"

"No, I ain't, Rose." Susan was not at the moment interested in Augustus Delfinney. "Rose what happened? I seen you running and all them boys chasing and I seen that Mr. Delfinney come after. I was some scared. I went to the missus where I was working and I got my pay and some other things and I hiked along the way I seen you run. Then I seen the boys come back and it wasn't long before he comes along on his horse and he said, 'Yes, I believe you're the young lady I'm looking for, come along up here.' I started to run and he laughed and come up close and whispered that he knew where my brother was and he seemed a nice man and I come and here I am. What did you do?".

"Have you got anything to eat in there?" Rose asked faintly, pointing to the bundle.

Susan had. She had bread and cheese, meat, tomatoes, two cold potatoes and two pieces of pie. She also had a bar of soap, a shirt and a pair of britches and boots, all well worn but still serviceable.

"I asked for 'em instead of some of the money," said Susan. "I took 'em for you." There was a warmth in the way she said it, and a kind of shyness, that made Rose look questioningly at her. Without another word being spoken, Rose understood that everything was all right again between them. She sighed.

Susan started to laugh. "Oh, my, but you do look a sight!" she said.

"Never mind," said Rose. "Give me the dinner." She sat down and ate and only afterwards did she tell Susan what had happened at the blacksmith shop.

Three nights later, refreshed, washed, neatly clothed, well fed, and with money in their pockets, the girls sat on the train as it pulled into the station in New York City.

Rose could not talk for the excitement that had come over her. There was a lump in her throat that felt as big as a rubber ball, her heart was pounding and she broke out alternately in hot and cold sweats. This was the end of the journey. After New York everything would be easy. Nothing bad could happen any more. New York was her home ground. As the train jerked to a stop and the conductor bawled out, "New York Central Station! Everybody change! New York Central Station! Everybody out!" she beamed at Susan, grabbed her hand and pulled her to the front of the line and out into the station.

The station was bigger, brighter, the crowd was thicker and there was more noise, but it was otherwise exactly like the ones at Oswego, Syracuse, Albany, and Poughkeepsie where they had got on that afternoon. Over the shouts of the hawkers, a man with a megaphone was calling, "This way to the horse cars! Come along ladies and gentlemen! This way to the downtown depot. Connections to Philadelphia, Baltimore and Washington. This way to the horse cars!"

Rose stood absolutely still as the realization sunk in. This wasn't Grand Central Station, not the Grand Central Station she knew with the information desk in the centre, the big electric signs at one end and, she looked up, the star-covered ceiling.

This was another station in another time, in Susan's time, in Mrs. Jerue's time, in Peter Maas's time. It wasn't the New York she knew.

She looked around wildly, refusing to believe what she saw. She began to shake and grew dizzy and cold, her knees gave out, there was a roaring in her ears. Then — blackness.

NEW YORK

As if from far away, voices came at her like sounds in a whirling wind, rushing near and fading again, saying nothing intelligible. Then Susan's voice, anxious, close to her ear. "Rose, Rose."

For a second, Rose thought she was back in the orchard at Hawthorn Bay. She opened her eyes slowly. "Poor kid," someone was saying, "I suppose it's the heat. Children shouldn't be out on their own at night like this. Pretty little boy, ain't he?"

Then an arm thrust itself through the crowd and a quiet, authoritative voice said, "Drink this." It was water in a tin cup. Rose sat up, and drank it. She smiled self-consciously at Susan who was gripping her hand as though she dare not let go.

"I'm all right." She wished they would all go away. "Really, I'm all right." She stood up carefully.

"Have you had any supper?" It was the woman whose arm had proffered the water, a tall woman dressed in grey with a big red face and kind eyes.

"I think so, I don't remember." She remembered leaving the shelter they had found after running away from the village of Dorland, the train ride, the excitement about coming to New York and the hideous shock of finding out that New York Central Station was not the Grand Central Station she had been expecting.

Ignoring the kind woman, who was offering to buy them supper, she said urgently to Susan, "We can't stay here."

"I know," Susan agreed. "We got to find that place you said would hold our grip and our money and get going."

Rose looked at her blankly.

"We got to get our suitcase and our money from that place you said keeps things that gets left on the train," Susan repeated patiently.

The crowd around had dispersed except for the tall woman who intervened once more to ask what the problem was. As briefly as possible, Susan recounted their misadventure on the train.

"Poor children," said the woman. "You shouldn't be travelling alone like this. I doubt very much if anyone has turned in either your grip or your money but, if you'll wait here, I'll go and enquire for you."

She was back in a few minutes during which time Rose sat as one under a spell. Her mind refused to work. Susan sat by her, peering anxiously into her face.

"I'm afraid no such grip has been turned in," said the woman, "and of course no money. I haven't much but I can give you enough for your evening meal."

"We got money," Susan assured her.

"You'll be all right then." The woman sounded much relieved. "I have to catch a train so I can't stay with you any longer. You'll be fine now, child. God bless you and bring you home safely." With a smile and a nod, she was off, a tall serene presence amid the noise and confusion of the station.

"Rose," Susan was saying desperately, "our grip is gone. It's like that Joe Haggerty said, we wasn't likely to find it nor our money. All the same, we got this far and we got some money and you know the way from here, so, like you always says, what we have to do now is get going."

Rose followed Susan like a robot through the station. They found a little horse-drawn bus that took them to the downtown depot at Chambers Street where they expected to get the midnight train for Washington. There they learned that the train left from Jersey City on the other side of the Hudson River. They would have to take another bus and a ferry to get there.

Rose would not go. She sat down on the nearest bench. "We'll be in Washington first thing in the morning, if we go on now," Susan urged. But Rose wouldn't budge.

"If you won't go tonight then we'd better get us a bite of supper," said Susan.

"You go."

"It's because of them things you lost in the bag, ain't it? That's what's wrong."

Rose had completely forgotten her treasures — her book, and her music box. She didn't care about them. They were treasures from a world that suddenly seemed very far away. There was no comfort even in their memory.

Susan sat down beside her and tried to coax her to come and eat, but Rose still would not move. Susan would not leave her so they stayed where they were; before long her head was nodding, she slumped down on the bench and slept.

Rose sat straight and unblinking. The shock had passed leaving her filled with dark, unreasoning terror. Her entire sense of what was real and what was not had been shaken. The feeling of being in a dream, that had started on the schooner on Lake Ontario, had made even the worst of the things that had happened bearable. But it had fled the instant she had set eyes on the inside of New York Central Station. Why she had expected to see Grand Central Station, familiar, twentieth-century Grand Central Station, she did not know, but she had. And now the world was shifting and changing around her and there was nothing to hold on to. An image flashed in her mind from a science-fiction movie she had seen, the image of a man hurled from his spaceship out into the black void. And there he would be rolling and tumbling through black space for all eternity. She shuddered.

After a while her senses began to settle, and as they did the world became real to her as it had never seemed real before. Colours were brighter. Smells were stronger. Sounds were sharper. She looked around. She was sitting in the Chambers Street railroad depot in New York City in August, 1865. It was oak-panelled, with benches in rows for people to sit on, windows and a big clock at one end. There were not many people there, a young mother with a cranky baby at the end of the bench, three nuns in long black habits pacing up and down the room, an old man sleeping, and two young soldiers sitting across from them.

They looked very ordinary and, like all the people Rose had ever seen or even known, they had nothing to do with her. That special sense of belonging she had had when she had first come up through the root cellar into Susan's world was gone as completely as the feeling of being in a dream. She was just Rose, as ill-fitting in this world as she was in the one she had grown up in.

She stared down at her feet and they looked like someone else's feet. In the boots Susan had got in Dorland they were the feet of David, the boy she had told everyone she was. And the britches were not hers. And she wasn't Rose Larkin but this other person, this made-up brother of Susan's. Reality wavered again. Who was she now? She began to tremble. Then, suddenly, Sam's face flashed into her mind, round and earnest and kind as it had been that day in Oswego when they had sat on the wall talking. It was gone immediately, but it settled her again and she was once more solidly back in the station. Fear did not leave her entirely but it dwindled to that much more ordinary fear of being in a strange place, knowing there was no one but herself to rely on. She was scared and hungry and she wanted to go home. And home was not New York. It was Aunt Nan and Uncle Bob's home at Hawthorn Bay. She was sad she would never be able to tell Aunt Nan that she was sorry about the accident or talk to Sam or play with the twins. She saw Sam's face again, this time with great clarity. He was sitting at the kitchen table, concentrating on playing his mouth organ. The twins were across the table listening. Sam looked up, directly at Rose, and the image faded.

She sprang to her feet. "There's got to be some way

besides the root cellar to get home!'' she almost cried aloud. "If I went to our old apartment on East 68th Street maybe I could do it. Maybe you can shift in places where you live?'' She looked down at Susan.

In her sleep, Susan had slumped over into a crumpled heap of dusty clothes, dishevelled hair and a pale face all streaked with coal dust and dirt. Rose sat down. "It was because of me we came here,'' she told herself. "Susan came because I said we had to. She thinks I can take care of everything." She pushed her hair back from her face. In the two weeks they had been on the road it had grown so that it was hot over her forehead. She put her face down in her hands. She knew that even if it was possible to find her way back to the twentieth century by finding East 68th Street she was not going to do it. She had to go with Susan to Washington, to find Will, and what was more she had to do it without letting Susan know how scared she was.

All night long she sat and thought. She thought of Will, who had become in her imaginings like all the soldiers she and Susan had seen. She could picture him all too vividly, maybe without an arm, or worse, his legs. She forced her mind away from Will, emptying it of those terrible pictures, and Aunt Nan moved in, ill in bed, the baby having died. She could not stand that so she thought of her grandmother, trying to remember how strict and cold and distant she had been, and all she could remember was how they had played checkers together and in a burst of longing she missed her grandmother sharply. Every thought she turned from led to another more painful. She got up and paced around and around the room until dawn finally came through the high dusty windows.

Susan woke up. They found that, for ten cents, they could have a wash basin and a toilet so they squeezed themselves into one small booth and helped each other wash off the dirt from the day before. Then they went looking for breakfast.

"Two dollars and fifty cents is a terrible price," the woman behind the counter of the buffet apologized. "I don't think it's right but with butter fifty cents the pound . . . ."

"We can't pay no two dollars and fifty cents for breakfast," said Susan, and Rose, as anxious as Susan to make their money last, looked hungrily at the sizzling eggs and beef and bacon but did not argue.

They found out that the train for Washington left the Jersey City station at eight o'clock and that they could take the six forty-five ferry from the Liberty Street dock. There was a horse car but they decided to save the money and walk. They had a quick cup of coffee and a bun which they bought at a stand near the entrance. Rose turned to Susan and announced firmly, "So the thing to do, Susan, is to get going." And Susan said, "That's so, Rose," and they set out.

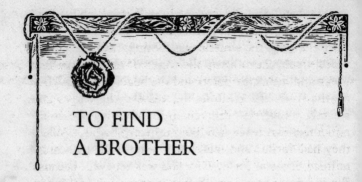

TO FIND
A BROTHER

It had rained in the night, and the morning sun shined up the cobbles on the street and made the iron knobs of the hitching posts that stood in a row in front of the depot look like polished ebony sticks. The mingled odours of fresh rain, horses, coffee and cooking from the food stalls was strong and not unpleasant. Sparrows were twittering and hopping along the street after the horses, pigeons strutted, one eye always on the lookout for crumbs. Already at six-thirty hawkers were shouting their wares and beggars clinked their tin cups.

Rose looked around her apprehensively. The fear that had overwhelmed her in the night still threatened. She wanted and she didn't want to know what the city was like. As they hurried along the streets she tried not to remember the Chambers and Greenwich and Liberty streets she knew, that were like dark tunnels smelling of garbage and exhaust fumes from the cars and huge trucks that were always squeezing past each other. She concentrated instead on the wagons and carts and carriages that rumbled past the office buildings, stores, hotels, and private homes — none of them over six storeys high. She did not let herself think about East 68th Street. When they reached the ferry docks, bells were clanging, the whistle was tooting, the huge paddle wheels were churning up the water. There was nothing to remind her of the docks and the boats she knew; out on the river, the great sailing vessels, the barges and steamboats were so different from anything she could remember that it seemed like a different harbour. When they had docked and made their way to the big, dingy railroad depot in Jersey City she was relieved, because she had never been there before so there was nothing in her memory to compare it to.

By this time the girls were seasoned travellers. They bought their tickets, two sandwiches and a square of gingerbread for their lunches, and found their train in short order. With the trauma of New York behind her, thoughts of Will came rushing in again. They were nearing their journey's end and fears assaulted her, fears that could be kept remote while there were still many miles to travel, and the travelling itself could occupy all thought. Would they find him? Would he be terribly changed? Would he be wounded? Sick? What if they could not find him? She could not bring herself even in her own mind to form the question: Would he be dead? She looked over at Susan sitting silently in the seat beside her, her eyes closed, and wondered if she too was afraid. She did not want to ask.

It was not long before exhaustion had taken over and Rose put her head against the windowsill and slept. When she woke the train was pulling out of a station and Susan was nudging her anxiously.

"I ain't sure where we are."

Rose rubbed her eyes, and sitting up saw a row of tidy houses with painted shutters and polished white steps, then a long, open vegetable market. In the distance was a tall bell tower. "What did the conductor say it was?"

"He said something that sounded like Filaleldelf."

"Philadelphia?"

"Yes."

"Well, if he didn't say Washington I guess it isn't time to get off."

"Rose, you know I couldn't ever have done this without you." Susan smiled at her warmly. "I think you're wonderful brave."

"No, I'm not. Really. I'm not," Rose answered, surprised.

"Yes, you are. You was brave to come and you was brave to stick when things got bad. I expect you could have gone back to wherever you come from any time you wanted and you didn't. You worked for that awful blacksmith and then, in New York, you never said nothing about losing all your things."

All Rose could think was how she had spent their last twenty cents in Albany, how she had wanted to leave in the Chambers Street depot, how mean she had been. "I wish I hadn't spent the money," she said.

"I wish I hadn't have left the grip with your things in it on the train."

"I don't care about them any more. You lost all your money. Susan, are you still angry with me?"

"Oh, Rose, after all you done!"

"But are you?"

"No, I ain't."

"Then I'm glad about everything else." Rose smiled and fell asleep again.

Susan woke her at the outskirts of Washington. The land was low and flat and they could see the Capitol dome rising above the church spires in the distance. As they approached the city they passed several acres of tents. The conductor told them they were army hospitals.

"Last year there were tent cities almost clear back to Baltimore," he said. "There are a few regiments still here because of the president being shot but most are gone. Even the hospitals are dwindling fast. Soon as a feller can walk, he goes home — unless of course he ships off to Arlington."

"Arlington?"

"Robert E. Lee's old estate, the new government cemetery, miss."

The conductor moved on, leaving the ominous sentence hanging in the air.

It was early evening when they reached the depot. "I ain't sleeping on no train station bench tonight," declared Susan. "And what's more I want a wash up. We got enough money for a room if it ain't too dear." They asked the ticket agent where they might find a place.

"Well, you turn out to be a pair of lucky youngsters," he told them. "It just so happens that my sister, a good Christian woman from Massachusetts, runs a boarding house over on 7th Street. The widow Fiske. Her house is right behind Brown's Indian Queen Hotel over near the stage and steamboat office. You can't miss it." In case they could, he repeated the directions three times and finished by saying, "Tell her Harold said you should come."

They had about half a mile to walk to Mrs. Fiske's

boarding house. Washington was unbearably hot, even in the evening, and it was damp and full of flies and mosquitoes. Washington did not frighten Rose the way New York had but it felt strange — alien. The trees had all been cut down, and the dirt streets were crowded with people, dogs, cats, cows, chickens, goats and pigs. The dust flew up in all directions with every passing carriage and cart.

"At least it ain't that awful black coal dust," said Susan, wiping her face with a filthy cloth that had been a clean white handkerchief only a day earlier.

"What difference does it make?" asked Rose. "I didn't know a person could get so hot and dirty and still be alive. There's coal dust and dirt in my teeth still. There's coal dust and dirt in my hair. I bet there's coal dust and dirt in my belly button and I know there's coal dust and dirt right through my skin and in my veins. I can't tell any more if I'm a white person or a black person."

"Shsh! Rose! They'll hear you! There's so many of 'em. I thought there was a lot when we was in Syracuse but here there's hundreds."

"Hundreds of what?"

"Shsh! Black people. Where did they all come from?"

"From the south I suppose. They were probably slaves and they came here to be free when Abraham Lincoln gave his emancipation proclamation. Why don't you ask?"

"Rose!" Susan was shocked. She grabbed Rose's arm and hurried her on.

By this time they were turning into Pennsylvania Avenue. The White House with its deep lawns was away to the south. As they turned north to go up the hill, the Capitol building was in front of them, its dome gleaming in the late sunlight. Rose remembered her one visit to Washington with her grandmother, a fuzzy memory of vast white buildings, wide tree-lined streets, parks and the huge statue of Abraham Lincoln. This Washington, with its dirt streets, animals roaming untended along them, and raw ugly tree stumps along the avenue, was like a dream turned inside out. She shivered and felt again that edge of dark fear.

"It's nice," Susan was saying, not realizing how Rose felt. "Them palaces is beautiful but the rest looks a sight more homely than New York. But there ain't been so many soldiers any other place."

So many soldiers — soldiers everywhere they looked. Like Susan, Rose peered anxiously into every face, hoping that by some lucky chance one might turn out to be Will's. The soldiers, so many of them disfigured, without an arm or leg, made her shudder. In their weary eyes, she saw the pain and hardship of the war they had just fought.

They did not find Will but they did find Mrs. Fiske's boarding house. Mrs. Fiske herself came to the door, a tall woman with black hair done in a tight knob on the top of her head. Sharp black eyes stared down a long nose at them. Her mouth looked to be permanently pursed in disapproval. She wore a black dress with a white apron over it, and when she talked she jingled the keys that hung from a chain pinned to her apron. They told her they had come to look for their brother Will.

"Well, don't stand there." Her voice was shrill and a bit nasal. "If Harold says I should take you in, then I'll take you. Lord be praised, I'm not a one to shirk my Christian duty. Follow me!''

She turned a brisk back and Rose and Susan followed it down a long dark hall that smelled of old cabbage and something they found out later was okra. They were led out through a back door into a yard where two black people were mixing dough and husking corn.

''You, Sally, and you, John,'' said Mrs. Fiske. ''Fetch up water for a bath and laundry.'' At her words, they put down their work and went swiftly into the house.

Mrs. Fiske turned to Rose and Susan. ''The Lord don't like dirt. You'll have to scrub and scrub good. You brother and sister?''

''Yes,'' said Rose.

''Then you can have the same tub. When you're done you wash up them dirty clothes. I'll get you clean ones to use while they dry. Then come to me in the kitchen. You can leastways make yourselves useful — charity can only go so far.''

''We ain't charity,'' said Susan stiffly.

''We're orphans,'' interrupted Rose, ''we're not used to charity, but we thank you very much.''

Mrs. Fiske's glance barely softened as she looked at Rose. ''You seem to know how to be grateful for the Lord's bounty, son,'' she said. ''Now scrub up smartly.'' She turned and went back into the house.

''Why'd you have to say that?'' whispered Susan fiercely as soon as Mrs. Fiske was out of sight. Her face had turned bright red and she looked very angry. ''We ain't charity. We got money.''

''We don't have that much money, Susan. She's horrible but she's going to let us have a bath and clean clothes and a place to sleep." Rose knew how to reach Susan. "And what if, when we find Will, he hasn't got any money?"

"That's so," said Susan, and they sat down on the grass and waited.

In a very few minutes, John and Sally came out of the house carrying a huge boiler between them.

"Y'all come along here with us." John nodded in the direction of a little wooden hut at the back of the yard. Inside was a large wooden tub in the middle of the floor, and a bench along one side. After Sally and John had poured the steaming water into the tub and enough cold water from the well out in the yard so that they would not scald themselves, Sally gave them a large chunk of soap.

"Theah, now," she said with a big smile, "y'all take off them filthy clothes and give 'em ta me. I'll scrub 'em up for ya, and Mrs. Fiske ain't never gonna know who done it."

They thanked her, and after Sally and John had gone outside they peeled off their clothes. "Black people is nice," said Susan and they got into the tub, gasping at the shock of the hot water. It smelled of steam and wet cedar wood and strong lye. When they were both sitting down, all squinched up together, their weight pushed the water so high only their heads stuck up above it.

Rose sighed. "I think this is the most blissful thing I've ever done in my whole life," she murmured. "If I die right here in this old tub full of hot water I won't care."

They washed their bodies and their hair and emerged from the blackened water like two new pink babies.

They dried themselves on the large cloth Sally had left and put on the clean clothes they found in a pile outside the door.

For Rose there was a pair of worn, slightly too small britches very like the ones she had taken off, only made of washed-out grey cotton, and a white shirt, much patched, a little big and still smelling of the iron. For Susan there was a dress, made of the same dull grey cotton, but neat with a small round white collar, and underdrawers. They found no stockings so they put on their shoes without. There was no comb or brush so they smoothed out their hair as best they could with their hands and went to look for Mrs. Fiske.

The kitchen smelled of roasting chicken. In the centre there was a large table covered with vegetables in various stages of preparation. Mrs. Fiske looked the girls over briefly, praised God for their new-found cleanliness and handed them each a pile of plates with instructions to put them at either end of the big table in the dining room — and be smart about it. For half an hour they carried plates of food to the twelve non-charity boarders, while Mrs. Fiske carved meagre portions from two chickens.

When the boarders had finished, Mrs. Fiske sat Rose and Susan down at the kitchen table, handed them each a small plate of vegetables, and recited a long blessing over them. "Now you be quick about eating as there's washing up to do." She left the kitchen.

As soon as she had gone, Rose jumped up and went over to where the remains of the roast chickens stood on a small side table, and without saying a word, picked over them until she had a handful of bits and pieces for the two of them.

After supper they washed the dishes for the twelve boarders. (Mrs. Fiske came in once to put away the remains of the chicken, looked at them very suspiciously and put it in a cupboard with a lock on it.)

It was after midnight when they finally got to bed in a little hot dark room over the kitchen. But they were up before the first sunlight and out of the house. They could hear humming from the kitchen and found Sally there getting the day started. She and John, it turned out, did not live there. They came every morning at five to start work.

"Where y'all goin', honey?" she asked, and they told her about Will. Sally got out two extra large chunks of corn bread, and found some cheese. "Now you hush up about this," she warned. Then she told them as much as she knew about the hospitals in Washington, and set them on their way with good wishes and prayers for their success.

They tramped the length and breadth of Washington that day. First they went out to Eighth Street to the hospital that Mrs. Heilbrunner on the Oswego train had told Rose about. They talked to the adjutant there. No, he didn't know of any boys from the 81st regiment.

"Not too many leave here except to go to the cemetery," he told them, echoing the train conductor's words. "I'm sorry to have to say that, but it wouldn't do you any good for me to lie. Perhaps you'd better check out at Arlington before you wear yourselves out looking in hospitals."

"I ain't going to." Susan was adamant. "I ain't looking first in no graveyard."

The adjutant passed them on to the matron who told them they could search through the hospital because there were soldiers there whose memories had gone, whose names no one knew.

They walked up and down the rows of cots looking into suffering, sick, and dying faces, bearing the smell of medicine, rotting flesh and bad food as long as they could. Will was not there. When they left, Rose vomited behind the building.

At the hospital they had learned the addresses of others. They went to all of them. No one knew Will or Steve, though they asked wherever they could, walked through long hospital wards, forcing themselves to look into each face. No Will, no Steve. By the time they had been through the third hospital, Rose longed to stop, longed never to look again into those faces, never to set foot inside one of those places of misery. Nothing that had happened to her, nothing she had ever imagined was like this kind of suffering. She was on the verge of telling Susan that she could not bear it any more, but one look at Susan's white face, the grim determination in her jaw, and Rose swallowed back the words, took Susan's hand and went on.

The heat was overpowering. Outside, the flies and mosquitoes were thick as the dust. Away from the stench of the hospitals, the air stank of sewage and catalpa trees. The heat shimmered on the roads. They stopped once to buy "ice-cold water" from a street vendor — but it was not, it was warm as bath water. Rose developed a large blister on the heel of one foot but she said nothing — about that or anything else. They were silent and resolute the whole day.

They took a horse car to go out to the tent hospitals, four in a row, and no word of Will or Steve there either.

One man from upstate New York was delirious and raving about mayflowers. Susan leaned over him and brushed the hair back from his forehead. "It might be Will," she said quietly.

"It isn't Will."

"It's someone's Will."

They took the car back into town. When they reached Mrs. Fiske's she already had dinner on the table. She fed them bread and thin soup in the kitchen.

"The Lord's great bounty has to be worked for," she told them severely and prayed over them for half an hour while the soup got cold, that they might be forgiven their selfishness when the Lord's work was waiting to be done. They said nothing to her, washed the dishes and went to bed. Early the next morning they found that Sally had left their own clothes on a bench in their room. They changed, crept down to the kitchen, helped themselves to two large corn muffins and sneaked out the front door.

"I don't mind the work," said Susan grimly, "but I can't abide a cold Christian. That ain't what the good Lord meant us to be."

That day was very like the one before. Each hospital they went to someone knew of at least one more they might try. Many nurses were sympathetic, and many convalescent soldiers wanted them to stop and talk, but all of them, some gently, some rudely, told them they ought to look in the Arlington cemetery before they wasted any more time looking in hospitals.

Worn out and discouraged, they slept that night in the front room of a little hospital in a building that had been a bank. Susan would not go back to Mrs. Fiske's. In the morning she helped the nurses. Rose could not face dressing wounds. She went into the kitchen. "I'm very good at washing dishes," she said.

"How are you at carrying trays?" asked one bright-eyed girl, thrusting a tray of porridge and toast and coffee into Rose's surprised hands. She carried the trays to the soldiers in their beds until the job was done, then started collecting them again.

"You reminds me of a young soldier we had here a while back," said a grey-haired man leaning back against his pillow, smiling wanly at Rose. "You walks with the same do-or-die attitude what he had — you and your sister there." He inclined his head towards the next bed where Susan was dressing a bandage. "Come to think of it, he talked like her, not like you. He come here with a comrade and he nursed that boy as loving as a mother until the boy died and the poor feller was so struck by his dying he never went home. He never said much to no one, he just stayed on helping out and growing more and more miserable and thin, till it looked like he'd die too."

Susan looked up. "Where's that feller now, mister?" she asked in a quiet, tense voice.

"I dunno, miss. Seems t'me I heard tell he'd gone on to another hospital. There was a nurse here was powerful good to them boys and she left here. I believe he went with her."

"Where would that be?" Susan persisted.

"I dunno, miss. Maybe Matron knows."

When she had finished her work, Susan went into the little front room that served as an office for the matron and asked her what she knew about the young soldier who had stayed to work and gone on to another hospital. Rose stood in the doorway, listening.

"I did hear something about that," said the matron. "It was before I came here. A young fellow, just a boy, so shattered by the death of his friend that he lost his memory or something."

"Where might he be now, ma'am?"

"You think he might be the boy you're looking for?"

"Might be."

"I see. Well, girl, you might go over to Georgetown and try there. There are a couple of small hospitals there, and I think one of the nurses from here went to Georgetown." The matron gave Susan directions and they left quickly. They said nothing to each other during the half-hour trip to Georgetown in the horse car, or walking the short distance to the hospital.

At the hospital, they found a tired-looking elderly woman. In a low voice, Susan asked about Will and Steve and told her the story that had been told them that morning.

"Just a minute," the woman said, "wait here." And she went off inside the hospital.

When she came back moments later, she said, "I'm not sure. I'm not a regular nurse at this hospital. I'm here only because my niece came down with typhoid fever. I've just come this morning. I don't have the names of any of the patients and I can't even ask as the men here are all in a very bad state. There's only one other nurse here now and she's sleeping. But there's certainly no boy like the one you describe. I really can't tell you any more than that."

Susan turned away from the door, and said, staring

straight in front of her, "I guess we got to go out to the graveyard." Her face was expressionless.

Mutely Rose nodded. She asked directions and within a few minutes they were on the road to Arlington.

It was only a mile and a half across the Potomac River and up a long hill. They did not speak and they did not look at each other. They stopped for a moment at the foot of the hill — they could see the Arlington cemetery above them. A solitary figure was coming through the gate. They walked slowly, quietly, up the hill, watching him come towards them. As he drew level, they saw he was a soldier. Suddenly Susan stopped. She drew in her breath sharply.

"Hello, Susan," said the soldier.

"Oh, Will," said Susan, "you got so thin."

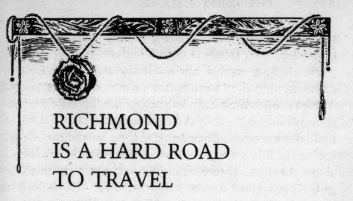

RICHMOND
IS A HARD ROAD
TO TRAVEL

Susan and Will stood staring at each other stupidly. Will moved forward a step. "Steve's dead," he said.

"I know."

The next moment Susan had her arms around Will and he was sobbing.

Rose stood back watching — not knowing what else to do. She was bewildered by finding Will like this and by the strangeness of him. Although she had seen him the day he had gone off to war, her memory of him was as he had been that day they had spent together in the boat and the orchard, a day that now seemed like three years past not only in Will and Susan's lives but in hers. This Will was not only tall, over six feet, but his ruddy face had become pale as parchment and he was thin and he looked so old. An old man, and Susan had her arms around him and he was sobbing.

After a time, Susan took Will by the hand as though he were a small child and led him to the bench by the cemetery gate where they sat down. He sat very still, holding tightly to Susan's hand. He looked up.

"Hello, Rose," he said. "There you are."

"Yes, it's me."

"What you said was true about where you come from."

"Yes."

"You ain't got any older."

"No."

"I guess it don't matter none."

Will turned back to Susan. "You was right," he said, "you was right, it wasn't no good." He began talking in a low, tired voice. "I never once took sick, but Steve, he got shot up at Cold Harbor right soon after we joined up and then, when he took sick after Petersburg, he was weakened and he never got shut of the sickness." Will paused and looked down at the ground. "He was a year younger than me."

"I know," said Susan, "I know. You want to tell what happened, Will?"

Quietly Rose went over and curled up under a tall yew tree that stood at a little distance from the bench where Will and Susan sat.

Will began again in that same low, tired voice, almost as though he were reciting a story he had learned by heart and did not want to tell but felt he had to. "We joined up in Oswego and we was plenty scared but we was pretty bucked up about it too. 'We'll get to Richmond and show them Johnny Rebs who can leave this country and who can't!' That's what Steve said. I remember him saying it as we marched down the street towards the recruiting office on West Bridge Street. They wasn't too particular about how old we was as they was getting pretty desperate for men by that time. The sergeant at the desk was a big-shouldered feller, with bristly black hair and beard, the kind that looks like a logger no matter what he does and he said we was fine fellers and how glad Uncle Sam was going to be to have us fighting for him. We was so proud and excited we was likely to bust. I said I knew the fife as I figured it couldn't be so different from the flute, and Steve said he knew the drum — Steve, he always figured he could do anything he set his mind to — and most always he could too. The sergeant said we was to join the 81st Infantry and he give us money and train tickets and uniforms.

"I remember the day was grand. You mind it was early May and the trees was in bud. The sky was blue as a bluebird's wing that day and there weren't no clouds at all. It was warm — awful warm for them uniforms but we didn't care. We put 'em on straight away and marched us down to the train station with the sweat pouring down inside, and Robert E. Lee himself couldn't have made us take off them coats. You know, Steve was almost a foot shorter than me but them quartermasters couldn't really see no difference, the uniforms was the same size, a mite small for me and a good bit big for Steve. We didn't even mind that and when we got down to camp in Virginny we made trades with fellers that had our size.

"We took the train from Oswego to Washington and then we went by boat to West Point in Virginny. It was pretty swell. People was always cheering us on and giving us grub and smiling and waving. We felt pretty near on top of the world. At West Point we was to get our training. They didn't need no fifers, nor no drummers neither, so we was made just ordinary soldiers and, what's more, we wasn't there much more than a week before we was needed so bad in the regiment we was declared trained. Steve was wild to get started. As soon as we got to Virginny we found out that the 81st had been fighting at Proctor's Creek and Drewry's Bluff and that them places was only a few miles from Richmond.

" 'They'll get there before we ever even get going,' he kept saying. Ever since he'd read that story about putting the first American flag up over Bennington Hill in the revolution in 1776, he'd dreamed of being a soldier and raising the flag for the country. And all the way down on the train he'd say, 'We're going to put that flag up over Richmond, Will. I know it! I know it! We're going to put that Old Glory up over that city and I'm going to be the boy that does it!' And he was scared, really scared the army'd get there before he got to be in it. But they didn't. They didn't.''

Will fell silent. His words hung in the still afternoon air like drops of water in a spider's web, fragile. His voice was so quiet, they barely heard him when he began again.

"It wasn't more than three days before we was in battle at Cold Harbor. Cold Harbor was something I never even had nightmares about beforehand to give me any kind of an idea of what it could be like. Even the old veterans said it was the worst battle they'd ever seen — worse than Manassas, worse than Chancellorsville, some said. It was hot as a bake oven and the dust stuck to your sweat like plaster and it was so thick you couldn't see who was friend and who was foe.

"And the Rebs was waiting for us on the field, all dug in their trenches nice and cosy and they shot us down as we moved in like we'd been a flock of pigeons. On the first day our regimental colours was taken. Captain Ballard and Captain Martin was killed and I think it was five other captains wounded from our regiment. Some said more than half the men and boys who started out that morning was left dead or dying on the field that night. Not just from our regiment but from the whole Eighteenth Corps. There was a fifer not more than nine years old lying dead near us.

"And it went on for twelve days. Twelve days! And in the nights, when we was frantically digging us trenches with anything we could get to hand, them mortars was flying over with their fuses like angry little red shooting stars through the blackness, and us never knowing where they was going to land. And the sound of battle never once let up — like some devil's music, the screaming bits of shell, the bullets and bars, the bugles blaring, the drums pounding, the horses and the men screaming.

"And the men dying. When they die, you know how they die? They jump. They shout. They cry. And they fall. You go into a rage and you want to get them devils who's shooting at you. That's all you think about. Then the battle's over for the day. The smoke and the dust starts to settle. The vultures — them big ugly turkey vultures — starts to wheel and circle around in the sky, looking for their dinners, and the smell of the dead is something awful. You look around and the rage is gone out of you and you don't hardly know yourself or your comrades neither.

"There's dead and wounded men lying all over the field, moaning and groaning, and those of us who wasn't hurt was trying to get them back to safety, and sometimes we could and sometimes them Secesh devils kept shooting and never once letting us near.

"Twelve days it was like that in them swamps and fields and briar patches. It was on towards the end Steve got shot. He was some fighter. I don't think he figured he could die. While the rest of us spent as much time crouching down in the trench like a bunch of scared ground hogs, Steve'd just put his head and his arms up and let fly with rounds of shot. We stayed together all the time so I was right beside him when it come, and he was so mad he was set to run right up out of the trench and get that black-hearted rebel who done it. I never stopped to think it through, I just hauled off and socked him in the jaw and put him out cold. I expect he would have got killed right there if I hadn't, and many's the time since I wished I'd have let him. But I guess what was at the back of my mind was that I wasn't going to go through the whole thing without him.

"He got shot in the arm right up close to the shoulder. Nobody thought too much about it, excepting to dress it, on account of there was so many so much worse off. Captain Raulston said he was a fine lad, and at the end of them twelve days in hell we was marched off to Petersburg, just south of Richmond. There was so few of us left after Cold Harbor — not a third of the regiment — there was only enough to make four companies. We hadn't the time to mourn, we was needed so bad, and three days later we was at Petersburg where the Secesh had their supplies defended.

"That General Grant he figured if we could cross the Chickahominy River and get to Petersburg we could knock down those defenses and starve out the Rebs.

Then we'd be in Richmond in no time. He just kept us going and going and going. We had a battle. We lost it. So Grant settled us all down in the trenches to see if we could starve them out. But we couldn't, and after a few weeks of that we was back in the Bermuda Hundred where the regiment had started from. I figure it was about that time Steve took the fever but he never let on — not even to me.''

Will stopped again. Susan said nothing but, even from where she sat under the yew tree, Rose could feel the comfort of Susan, patient and loving.

And there was comfort in the quiet afternoon, in the dappled shade of tall oak trees and the thicker shade of yew and cedar. Up beyond the gate, beyond the graveyard, was a white pillared mansion. It looked old and settled, almost as though it might have stood there forever. Down below the hill, the Potomac River flowed gently towards the sea and beyond it was the golden dome of the Capitol building. It would be night before Will had finished his story.

''And after a while'' — Will picked up his tale — ''it was as though there hadn't never been nothing but dust and filth, and bad sowbelly and beans and mush — and dying men. Steve took to it right off. He figured it was a good life even after he had the wound. I could never see how come he did but I guess Steve was like that. Even when we was kids he was always wanting to walk on the edge of cliffs or climb to the top of trees, or run into fields just to scare the bulls. Not me. I used to admire him an awful lot for being brave but I thought some of them things was foolish. All the same, when Steve was around doing those crazy things, everything seemed exciting, and when he talked about going to war, I felt the excitement too. I was so full of glory and halleluiah I had to go. But I never took to it like he did. All I could think was we had to win. I figured we had to save the country, but many's the long night I lay awake and just prayed for it to be over. And I never took sick and I never once got wounded — just tired of marching.

"Of course it wasn't all horrible. In the evenings we'd play crib and euchre. Somebody'd made a fiddle out of a cigar box and another feller had a mouth organ and we'd sing. Sometimes we'd go on foraging parties and swipe chickens — things we'd never dream of doing at home — only of course there wasn't much left to swipe in Virginny, mostly just berries to pick along the way where they wasn't burned out.

"We never got out of our dirty clothes from one month to the next and after a time we was crawling with lice.

"It felt like we'd been marching back and forth from one hot, dusty, burned-out spot in Virginny to another forever before I found out about Steve's sickness. We was sitting by the roadside finishing off a ration of hard-tack and camp coffee, and it was hotter than the flames of hell and the only breeze for miles around came from Tim Arepy whistling 'Rock of Ages' through his teeth. I remember Billy Nasset sitting down the way a piece, polishing off his coffee, getting up, stretching and belching, and saying in his big loud voice, 'Well so much for the steak and potatoes, where's the cake and ice cream?' and I looked over to Steve to say something and there he was, the colour of putty and shaking like a balm of Gilead tree in a high wind. And I realized, all of a sudden, that he'd been sick for quite a while — you know how it is sometimes when you find something out and you know you've really known about it for a long time? I stared and before I could say anything he turned his head and saw me looking at him and he knew I knew he was sick.

" 'You ain't to tell, Will,' he said. 'I ain't going to no hospital. I'm going to Richmond and put up that flag.' And he looked at me in that kind of way he had that had always got to me and always made me do things for him or with him I hadn't thought right or proper, or hadn't much wanted to do. So, being the kind of coward I am, I promised. And we went on. Sometimes Steve was bad and sometimes he seemed O.K., but as the summer went on he leaned on me more and more while we marched and many's the time we argued about taking him to hospital, but he always won. 'You promised, Will,' he'd say and I'd just have to give in. I'd have to go along though now I don't know why. He wanted it so fierce. And when we was sent up to New York in November, to help keep the peace in case there was riots during the election, he was scared out of his mind that he wouldn't make it back in time to get to Richmond when she fell. And all that winter he got sicker and sicker — much sicker than I knew because he kept himself going, God knows how. He'd just made up his mind he wasn't going to be too sick to fight, and somehow he stayed on his feet — most of the time anyways. But all the same he was changing. The fire in him was gone. He didn't talk much or make jokes any more and in some ways he was like a little kid. He'd say, 'Don't go on without me, Will,' or 'You won't leave me, Will? Don't go — stay here — wait for me — where are you going?' It was like he was using my energy to keep him going, and he was afraid to let me out of his sight. And I began to wish to God I could be shut of him for five minutes — just five minutes.

"Then one day I couldn't stand it. We'd come through the winter. It was March. Spring comes to Virginny in March like it comes in May up home, only the birds and the plants ain't all exactly the same. This morning it was fine, as fine a morning as I'd ever seen in my life. The cardinals was scolding in the holly bushes and them big magnolia flowers was in bloom, in a tree over by an abandoned farmhouse. I'd stood up, just to get myself a stretch and sniff the air, and Steve cried out straight away, 'Where are you going, Will?' and I just found myself shouting at him, 'Home. That's where I'm going, home,' and I run off. I had no idea where I was going, I just went.

"I ran and I ran until I come to a bit of a woods and a pasture beyond where there was a fence. Most of the fence had been taken away but back by this bit of woods there was just a piece of it left, all grown over with a wild ivy vine like them vines that grows around Bothers' fence up by the swamp. And there wasn't nobody there but me and I was come over sudden with such homesickness that I threw up.

"When I was done I got up and I stood holding on to an old oak tree with my arms tight around it and I bawled until I couldn't bawl no more.

"When I'd settled myself a little I thought about how awful it was, how mean of me to have run off like that and say I was going home. I wasn't going home. I let go the tree and headed back towards camp. Then I heard a rustling in the underbrush and in two seconds I was face to face with a desperate-looking feller and he had a knife.

"I wasn't never much of a boy to fight, you mind, even in games back home, though by this time I'd done plenty of it. I didn't want to fight but this boy had a knife. He was shorter than me by quite a good deal but wider and he looked strong. He had straight black hair, blacker than Steve's, and it was hanging around his dead-white face. His eyes was like black coals and they looked as though they'd kill me if they could.

"We took the measure of each other and I reached out quick and grabbed him by the arm that had the knife. He was quick and he made a pass at my face with that arm even though I had a hold of it. I ducked away and tried to grab hold of the other arm but he was too quick and he got a hold of my hair and he pulled. I kicked out and tripped him up, and over the fence we went, the both of us rolling in the nettles and grunting and panting and rolling over and over and over. And something in me that had been burning let loose on this black-eyed murderer and I kicked and grabbed and punched and held on to that arm that kept coming up to my eyes, my throat, my ribs, it must have been a dozen times.

"Once he grabbed me by the throat with the other hand and I think he would have won but we rolled down a little hill and into a creek. It surprised the both of us so much he lost his grip for a minute and he let go of my throat and the knife both at once. Now he was stronger than me though he was smaller but I didn't want to die and when I got the upper hand I let him have it. I punched him in the gut and I blacked his eyes, both of 'em, and punched his nose until it poured blood over both of us. Then I pounded his head until he cried out. Then I sat on him and we glared at each other, him with his eyes going blacker by the minute and me with the marks of his thumb on my neck.

" 'If y'all mean t'kill me, Yankee, get doin' it,' he said, and I looked him right in his black rebel eyes and I could see they wasn't but ordinary eyes, scared but brave too, and he wasn't but a boy, probably younger than me. I reached over into the creek where the knife was laying and I picked it up. I looked at it and I looked at him. I couldn't kill him like that, like slaughtering a chicken or a pig.

"I got up off him. 'Get up,' I told him and he did. I knew he was a rebel, he talked like one. But he didn't have no uniform on. He had on a pair of britches might have been made for a giant and they was tied on him with a string.

" 'You skedaddling?' I asked him.

"He didn't say nothing.

" 'Where you from?'

" 'Tennessee.'

" 'Is that where you're going?'

" 'I dunno.'

" 'Wherever you're going you better get there and fast.'

"He ran. I listened to him crashing through the woods and I never moved until not only the sound of him was gone but the birds and the squirrels had stopped scolding and screaming about it. Then I doused my head good in the creek. I kept his knife — still have it — and I went back to camp feeling better about everything.

"It wasn't long after that we moved into Richmond and the war was over. Our regiment was first into the city just like Steve had said right along it was going to be. It was the third of April, a Monday, not a day I'm likely to forget. We was camped outside the city the night before and all that night the city burned. The rebs had fired her up, lit up the arsenal and the whole city'd caught fire. When we marched in at eight o'clock in the morning there wasn't nothing but ruins right up to the capitol building.

"Like I said, our regiment was the first into the city and it was us that put up the first flag but it wasn't our company and it wasn't Steve though by that time he didn't much care. He was just glad to see it go up. We marched in right behind the company of coloureds that was first in. We marched straight to the prison where the Union soldiers was kept. We opened the doors and let them out, then we pulled down the rebel flag.

"Up went the Stars and Stripes and the fifer played 'Glory Halleluiah', and our boys was cheering and shouting so loud you could barely hear the music. And I looked at Steve's face. He was standing there, sort of leaning against me, looking at that flag and glowing like he'd seen an angel.

"And there was others the same, but not me."

Will stopped. He looked at Susan and, for the first time during that whole, long recital, his voice broke. "Susan," he said, "you was right. I stood there in Richmond. The rebs had gone. The town was all but burned right out. The war was almost done. I looked up at the flag going up over the Libby Prison, and it wasn't my flag. I listened to all them shouts and looked at all them joyful faced and I knew that what you said back in the orchard at home before I took off was true. It wasn't my war, Susan, it just wasn't my war.''

Will put his face down into his hands, and there was such an air of utter despair about him that Rose, listening under her tree, wanted to get up and put her arms around him. But the story he had told had been for Susan and the despair he was wrapped in could only be broken by her. Instinctively Rose knew that and stayed where she was.

After a few moments, Will sighed deeply and sat up straight.

''That night old Abe come in to Richmond to see how things was and, I expect, to cheer us on. He was a strange-looking man, like a couple of scarecrows set above one another to make one awful tall thin man with a high silk hat on top, but his face was something wonderful and, you know, Susan, the preacher would likely say I was blaspheming but I thought to myself that if I could paint a picture of the face of God that's how I'd make it.

''He walked right by me,'' Will was saying, ''not just when we was standing on parade but afterwards, when I was standing guard by the capitol building, and I couldn't stop myself — I reached out and touched his arm. He never noticed but I felt a gladness in me. And then, not two weeks later, on Good Friday, he was shot in that theatre by that crazy Booth. And you know, Susan, I felt as if the sun had got turned off. I never felt exactly like that even when my own pa died and Pa was a good man.''

Will turned his worn cap slowly around in his hands. ''There's not much more to tell after that,'' he said.

"We stayed in Richmond about a week, guarding the miserable ruins, trying to make some kind of order of them, and all the while we were there Steve got sicker and sicker. It was like he'd just given up once the flag was up over Richmond. We wasn't camped with our own company, God knows why. Things was just some mixed up and I don't know when our boys left the city. To tell the truth, the heart had gone out of me. All I could think was I'd gone through all that hell and it hadn't ever had nothing to do with me and worse, oh so much worse than that, if it hadn't of been for me Steve wouldn't have gone, not all by himself he wouldn't, and I was so sick at heart I was like to die. So I cleared us out. I got us on a boat going down the river. There's a song we used to sing that says Richmond is a hard road to travel, and all the way down the James River and up along the bay and into Washington, sitting on that deck with Steve lying with his head on my knees, all I could think was maybe it is but it ain't so easy coming back either.

"We'd passed through Washington on our way down from New York in November, and I remember what one of the boys said when he seen the White House. He said, 'It sure don't look much like a house I'd live in. I'd sure like to trade with old Abe a few days.' We'd all laughed and had a good time. But when we come back, Steve and me, it was a different kind of feeling. He was somewhere else in his head pretty near all the time by then and I just lived every day with this lump of fear at the bottom of my stomach. A captain from the New York 125th took us in charge and got us to the hospital. Steve never got no better. There was times he'd know me and sit up, his eyes sort of wild, and say over and over, 'Promise me, Will, you promise me you'll let me stay and get us into Richmond.' Other times he'd be back playing ball in Oswego or calling out for Aunt Min. Once, just once, he sat straight up and looked at me as if he'd known right along what was going on, and he said, 'Will, you ain't going to let me die?' and he grabbed me by the hand so hard all I could think to say was, 'No, Steve, I ain't,' but of course there wasn't nothing I could do about it and he died a week after that and the last thing he said was, 'Don't leave me, Will. Promise!' I don't know how long we was there and I don't know how long it's been since then. We buried him out here at Arlington and like I promised, I ain't left him alone. I stayed for a time at that hospital where he died, then there was this kind nurse that took herself over to the little place in Georgetown where all the dying fellows was and I figured I might as well go along. So I did.''

Will stopped at last. His face looked grim and very old. In the silence that followed his story, Rose realized that without having been aware of it she had been crying. Shakily, she wiped the tears from her face. But all she said was, ''Let's go home.''

I'M NOT
COMING HOME

Susan stood up, pulling Will with her. "That's what we have to do now," she said decisively. "We have to go home. Will, your ma's going to be some glad to see you."

"Susan, I ain't going with you."

"What?"

"I ain't going with you."

"What do you mean?"

"I promised. I promised Steve I'd stay by him."

"Will, Steve's dead."

"And if I hadn't have been so stupid he wouldn't be."

"Stupid? You mean because you promised you wouldn't take him to the hospital?"

"I should have taken him no matter what he said."

"But that don't mean because you promised something and it turned out wrong you got to keep another promise — especially when the person's dead."

"Yes it does. That's just what it does. Don't you see, I was kind of in charge of Steve. He was younger than me so I had to take care of him. And I let him die. The only thing I can do now for him is to keep my word to him."

"Will, ain't you had enough of the dead and dying? It ain't like you. You was always a one to love the living things. Remember how it was you who found the first trilliums in the woods in spring? And knew where the lady's slippers grew and wouldn't tell no one but me for fear someone would spoil 'em? And you was the one to help your pa with the lambing even when you was real small. It's them living things you belong to, Will. Steve's gone, and it's terrible sad but there ain't nothing you can do to bring him back though you sit here till you die at the age of a hundred or more. You'll go crazy like your ma."

"I ain't coming with you, Susan."

"Will, you have to come. Susan's right about when people are dead. They're just dead, and you can't do anything about that. I know," Rose said.

Will stared from Rose to Susan and back again. He stuffed his hands into his pants' pockets and paced back and forth swearing to himself. Then he started down the hill.

"I don't want to talk about it," he said harshly.

"Come on, we don't need to stay here all day."

In single file they walked towards the road. Out on the hillside there were fields of corn, and pastures where cows and horses were grazing. In the distance the late sunlight made a fairytale palace of the gold dome of the Capitol building. It was quiet and beautiful but none of them noticed. All three were thinking their own thoughts. They reached the road and, in silence, continued on towards the river, one behind the other like children playing follow-my-leader. Rose thought of the time she had told Susan about spending the money and

Susan wouldn't walk with her. In front of her, she heard a muffled sob. She quickened her step and caught up with Susan.

Susan's head was down and tears were running down her cheeks and chin, and making little muddy rivers down the front of her dress.

"Have you been crying all this time?" whispered Rose. Susan nodded. The tears went on falling.

"Is it because Will won't come? To think I worked a whole week for that hideous old gargoyle Peter Maas just so we could get here! I'm not giving up now! We'll find a way yet." Rose quickened her step and moved ahead to keep up with Will's long, marching stride.

"Susan's miserable," she said.

Will said nothing. Rose put her hand on his arm. He shook it off.

"She's crying," Rose repeated. "We came all this way to get you. You can't just say, 'I ain't coming,' and let us go all the way back to Hawthorn Bay, Canada, without you. We had a very hard time getting here."

No response.

"Will Morrissay, I think you must be the most stubborn person in all the world ——" she stopped. Will was looking down at her, and behind his tired eyes Rose could see the pain of where he had been and what he had seen. It was almost like a physical blow. Her first instinct was to shield herself from it. Then she wanted to shield Will. She grabbed his hand. She wanted to cry the way Susan was crying for Will, for Steve and all those others, for the horror of war which she didn't understand but felt the deep sadness of. She trembled from the grief that welled up inside her. But she did not cry.

She could not, because of the terror in the grip Will had on her hand. She understood about terror and she held on to him, willing herself to be as strong as he thought she was.

After a while Will realized he was holding Rose's hand in a crushing grip, and he let go and walked on more easily. By and by Susan moved up beside him and they walked along the river road, and through the streets to the hospital, three abreast, in unspoken companionship.

"I see you found him." It was the same woman who had opened the door to them earlier in the day. "I'll get Matron for you."

They went inside and, in a moment, a round, motherly-looking woman appeared. When she saw Rose and Susan with Will her face lit up.

"So," she said, "you've come to take my boy home."

"He won't come," said Susan.

Matron looked at Will who stared stubbornly back at her.

"I see," she said, and nothing more except, "I expect you're ready for your suppers."

Tiredly they ate cold beef and potatoes and corn in the kitchen. Will slept, as was his habit, on a cot just inside the door of the room where the sick and needy patients were: Matron found cots for Rose and Susan and put them in an upstairs room. The room had long windows in the front that looked out on the street and a high ceiling with plaster molding around it carved in the shapes of grapes and strawberries and melons and leaves.

"I bet it was a wonderful room when it had all its furniture and drapes," said Rose.

"I guess so," Susan said and, apart from whispering prayers to herself, she said nothing else. She curled herself into a tight ball like a kitten and after a time Rose heard her breathing deeply.

Rose lay watching the shadow of the house making arrows and angles in the moonlight across the foot of her cot. The images Will had put in her head were still fresh and sharp, and stronger even was the look she had seen in his eyes as they had walked together on the road from Arlington. She thought about Will, so weary and grieved, and the way he had been that day in the boat, so eager and full of delight. She remembered that she had thought about marrying Will. She thought about Susan who wanted only one thing, to have Will home, and about her own self not really knowing what she wanted or even who she was.

"Being a person's too hard," she thought, "it's just too hard."

She got up. She put her clothes on, and went downstairs, through the hall, through the long hospital ward where the men snored and groaned, and into the smaller ward behind it where Will slept just inside the door.

She leaned over and shook his arm.

He sat up, looking around him with quick, jerking movements, and reached for something beside his bed that wasn't there.

"Will, it's me, Rose. I want to talk to you."

He swerved around and focussed on her. He sighed in obvious relief.

"O.K." His voice was tired, full of resignation.

"I'll wait for you outside in the back, by the kitchen door."

"O.K."

The door out of the kitchen led to a small yard very
like the one at Mrs. Fiske's. Rose sat down on the
doorstep. The moon was high above the branches of the
catalpa tree that stood at the back of the yard and by its
light Rose watched a thin, mangy grey cat walk along
the top of the board fence that separated the yard from
the one next door.

Will came out and sat down beside her. He had two
cups of tea in his hands.

"Thanks," said Rose. "Will, you have to give me
some money."

"Some money?"

"Have you got some?"

"Yes, some."

"I want to go home. Susan won't come without you.
She'll stay here."

"No, she won't."

"Will Morrissay," said Rose, "you're a lot older than
I am now and you're a soldier and terrible things have
happened to you so I shouldn't say it but you're being
dumb. Or you just don't know Susan at all. She won't
go home without you. She'll stay here forever if that's
what you mean to do. But I don't want to. I want to go
home. I don't want to be stuck back in time. I'm sick of
being a ten-year-old boy. I want to be myself, ordinary
Rose with an ordinary Aunt Nan and an ordinary Uncle
Bob and ordinary cousins. I don't belong here — I
thought I did but I don't — any more than you belong in
the United States. I want to go home to Hawthorn Bay.
You know, I've just remembered something. A funny
man on the road from Albany asked me where I came

from. I said Canada, and I do now. Same as you. And I don't see any way of getting there except to take the train and the boat and I don't have any money. I want you to give me some.''

Will said nothing for a few minutes. He sipped his tea and watched the cat sharpen its claws against the fence.

''Would you give me some money?''

Will reached into his pocket and took out some bills. Rose took them and stuffed them into her pocket. ''Thanks. Oh, and this belongs to you.'' She pulled out the tiny cloth packet she had been carrying in her pocket since Susan had given it to her in exchange for her silver rose in the garden at Hawthorn Bay. ''It's your song.''

''My song?''

''The song you wrote about the bird and the day you and Susan and I were in the orchard.''

He frowned, took it from her, and opened it slowly. He stared at it as though it were the ghost of someone long dead and forgotten.

''My song,'' he said wonderingly, ''my song.''

Rose began to hum it as she had so many times to herself and to Susan. ''I wish you had your flute,'' she said when she had finished.

''Flute,'' said Will, in that same bewildered voice. He was looking at the worn, creased piece of paper. ''Flute,'' he said again. His hands were shaking. ''I lost my flute. I lost it at Cold Harbor. I didn't care. I didn't want to play it anyway. I didn't think there'd ever be any music in the world again except tramp-tramp-tramp and the dead march. After that I forgot. I forgot.

''But I remember now. I remember that day I made

the song. I wanted so bad to write it so I wouldn't forget.
I went to see old Mr. Lestrie down in Soames, who used
to teach music there. I asked him if he could show me
how to write it and he did. And he said he'd teach me a
lot more if I wanted but I never went again. I guess I was
scared. I was a kid. I thought you were wonderful.'' He
looked at her shyly. ''And all them things you talked
about. I thought a lot about all that after you disappeared and I couldn't figure it out. Then one day I seen
you, must have been a year or more after you'd gone. I
seen you out by the road. I was going to go and talk to
you but before I could you was gone. You was gone the
way a drop of water on a hot pan goes — just dries up
and ain't no more. It gave me the shivers but then I done
some more thinking and I figured that what you said
was true, every word.''

''But I didn't stay gone,'' said Rose and she felt happy.
''I came back. And Will, remember what you said about
belonging, that day in the orchard? Do you remember?
You said, 'It doesn't matter where you come from.' You
said, 'I guess what matters is where you belong.' Well, I
know now. I belong in that other time and I have to go
back there.

''I have to tell you something.'' Rose looked at Will
out of the corner of her eye, and quickly looked away. ''I
thought you were wonderful too. I decided I was going
to marry you.''

''What!''

''I was. I was going to marry you. But I know now
that it was silly because I'm not the one who is going to
marry you, and anyway I belong in another time, and I

have to go back even if I go by myself. I'm going to go down to the train station and go home.''

"Go back to bed, Rose," said Will, "and we'll all go together by and by."

Rose did not let him see her smile of satisfaction.

THE STORM

It seemed as though she had barely fallen asleep although it was an hour later when Rose woke to find Susan standing by her cot. When she saw that Rose was awake, Susan dropped to her knees and put her arms tightly around her.

"You done it," she whispered. "You done it. Like Will told you all that long time ago, you was good luck, the best luck a body ever had. Will told me what you talked about in the night. I love you, Rose."

Embarrassed by her own show of emotion, Susan stood up. "Matron's give Will some money she figures he's got coming to him for working here," she said, "so with what I got, and what Will give you, we got enough for all our fares and one good dinner."

"What about lemonade?"

They both laughed.

"Will and I, we been out to the graveyard to say our prayers over Steve," Susan went on, "and Matron says the morning train goes out of Washington at eight o'clock. So Rose, what we got to do is go get on the train."

"That's so, Susan." They grinned at each other. Rose

leaped out of bed and got dressed hastily. They ate a quick breakfast, said goodbye to Matron who said "God bless you" to them all but took Will in her arms as though she were his mother, adding "you have a good angel, you'll be all right now," and off they went. Rose wondered if Matron meant Susan or the other kind of angel.

When the train stopped at Philadelphia, Rose bought Will a harmonica for ten cents. He played it hardly at all at first, but after an hour or two he played it softly all the time, trying out notes, remembering notes, completely losing himself in the music.

Rose knew now that she wanted to go home to Aunt Nan and Uncle Bob and the boys but when she thought about leaving Will and Susan, especially Susan, she felt sad. "You won't forget me, Susan?" she pleaded.

"I ain't likely to."

Neither of them said any more about it but thoughts of parting hovered over them throughout the journey. They travelled all day, all night, and arrived in Oswego just after noon the next day. Will stepped off the train behind Susan and looked around him slowly in all directions. He sniffed the air.

"Looks like a storm's brewing to the west," he said. Otherwise, none of them said anything all the way to Mrs. Jerue's house.

Will knocked at the door. They stood three in a row and watched through the screen as Mrs. Jerue came towards them along the hall, her wide, flowered skirt bumping the walls. They saw her questioning look become a look of surprise, her surprise become a smile and the smile fade as she realized that the tall soldier with Susan and Rose was Will and that Steve was not with them. She opened the door. "Come on along in, Will. Thanks be to God for your safe home-coming." Then, though the tears began to flow down her face, she put her arms around Will and they hugged each other tightly.

The children had come running at the sound of voices, and at first there was a hushed and horrified silence. But Mrs. Jerue took them into her grief as generously as she had taken them into her house. She listened, with the children, to Will tell stories about Steve in the army, some funny, some sad, and then they all told stories about him, remembering all the things he had done in his life. They laughed and cried together, and Mrs. Jerue made a huge meal for them after which she insisted on hearing the tale of Rose and Susan's journey south. She scolded them both for running off.

"If you could have seen me." She sighed. "You know I'm not as slim as I once was and I had some terrible time. When Charlie here come running to tell me you'd run off, I figured pretty fast (my brain's not run to fat, you see) where you'd gone and we hightailed it down to the station just in time to see the train pull out."

"We saw you," confessed Rose.

"Why you young scallywags!" Mrs. Jerue chuckled. "You sure gave me a run around, but I suppose I wouldn't have it any other way now. It might have been we'd none of us ever have seen our Will again neither, if it hadn't been for you."

They spent a night and a morning at the Jerues'. The first night they bathed and Mrs. Jerue took away all their clothes. Early the next morning she came into the little room where Rose and Susan slept. She gave Susan a pretty pink and white flowered dress of Jenny's, and when Susan had put it on, Mrs. Jerue said, "Now run on along, girl, and get your breakfast." Then she sat down on Rose's bed and fixed her with a steady gaze.

"You come here with Susan and you spun us quite a yarn. Then you sneaked off. Where'd you come from, youngster?"

Rose squirmed inside Charlie's nightshirt that Mrs. Jerue had given her to sleep in.

"I don't much like being lied to," said Mrs. Jerue.

"I'm sorry." Rose's voice was very small.

Mrs. Jerue frowned. She leaned over and inspected Rose closely, the way she might have inspected cabbages for holes or bugs. "What's more, you ain't a boy," she declared.

Rose felt very uncomfortable for a moment; then, suddenly, she felt as though a burden had been lifted from her. "I'm Rose Larkin," she said. But how to tell Mrs. Jerue where she had really come from? She didn't want to lie. So she said, "I'm a friend of Susan's. I didn't want her to have to go find Will by herself. So we thought it would be useful if I dressed as a boy. And I guess it was, too. But I'm sorry we made you run after us to the railroad station."

"That's all right, Rose, it's all in a lifetime, as I always say. Now, you stay put for a minute." Mrs. Jerue left the room.

In a minute or two, she was back with a dress over her arm and a pair of boots in her hand. "There, this ought to do just fine for you. Louisa's grown out of it. It'll be dandy with your red hair."

The dress was white with grass-green stripes. It had mutton-chop sleeves, a high collar, and an ankle-length full skirt, not as full as the skirts Mrs. Jerue herself wore

— there was no hoop — but fuller than any Rose had ever worn. To go with it, there was a green velvet ribbon. "To tie up your hair, as it's some grown out since you was here before." Mrs. Jerue smiled, her tired eyes red from weeping. Holding the clothes tightly to her, Rose smiled back.

She was left alone to figure out the underdrawers and the petticoat, and to contort herself into impossible shapes as she struggled with the buttons at the back of the dress. She tied the ribbon around her head and smoothed the dress down carefully. "I like it," she whispered to herself as she looked down at the edge of lace that revealed the petticoat peeping out from beneath the skirt, and the high, buttoned boots on her feet, which were only the tiniest bit too large.

She went downstairs to where Will and Susan and the Jerue children were having breakfast. Will's eyebrows went up but he said nothing. The children stood and poked each other and whispered but said nothing either — except for Charlie. His mouth hung open and then he said, "You mean you worked for that mean blacksmith and everything and you're a girl!"

Susan smiled at her approvingly. Rose sat down and ate her breakfast.

Right after breakfast, Will went down to the wharves. He was back very soon. "The weather's growing more chancy by the hour," he told them, "but Jake Pierson's going out in about an hour and he'll take us if we want to go."

"If I was you, I'd wait out the storm right here," said Mrs. Jerue. Rose said, "No. We can't." She had a sudden fear. Now, when she had discovered how much she wanted to get back, she was afraid something would happen to keep her from getting there, that the storm would keep them away. She could not bear to delay.

"Jake's a pretty sound man." It was almost as though Will had read her mind.

"And you're pretty anxious to get on home." Mrs. Jerue sighed and took Will's hand. She offered no further arguments. She put on her bonnet, gathered her children and set out down the street.

The streets they walked were the same ones they had come along only three weeks earlier but there was a nip in the air on this morning, although it was only September. The women wore shawls and where they had ambled and sauntered before, they bustled and hustled along.

The *Sarah Maud* had been unloading barley all night and was being made ready to turn right around and head back to Hawthorn Bay.

"Jake Pierson's place is right up to the head of our bay," Susan explained to Rose, "so we're mighty lucky to find him here."

The wind was growing strong. Captain Pierson greeted Susan briefly, nodded at Rose, and showed them where they could berth. It was a smaller schooner than the one they had come over on, a two-master, with a smaller cabin for sleeping and cooking, and a crew of two.

"Frank March and Jim Bedell," Susan told Rose, "and that Jim's such a lazy one, Jake'll be right glad to have Will aboard."

Mrs. Jerue hugged Will long when it was time for goodbyes. "You be my boy, now, too," she said. Then

she gave Susan a big hug and a "God bless you, child,"
but when she turned to Rose, she shook her head.
"You're a funny one," she said. "There's more to you
than you told me, I'm certain sure. But if you ever come
back this way, you remember Min Jerue. There'll
always be a place here for you."

Impulsively, Rose threw her arms around Mrs. Jerue.
Then she shook hands with all the children.

"I'm sorry, Charlie," she said when she got to him,
"I didn't mean to spoil things for you."

"Do you want to be my girlfriend?" asked Charlie.
Rose was so taken by surprise she nearly laughed, but
she didn't. "I'd like to Charlie," she said, "but I can't
because I live too far away." Then she remembered
something she had heard someone say in a movie and
she told him solemnly, "I'm really much too old for
you, Charlie. But I will always hold your love in my
heart," and she turned and went away without waiting
to see what effect her words had had on Charlie.

"Cast off," the captain shouted and Will and the
other two young men let loose the lines and, pulled by
the tug, they were soon out in the open lake, their sails
set.

"The wind's from the south," Will called to Rose
happily, "so we won't be no time at all getting home."
And it looked as though they would not be. The sky was
grey but the heavy clouds were scudding across with the
wind, like banners leading the way. Within six hours,
they were within sight of the island shore. But then the
wind shifted a little to the west, the clouds thickened
and turned black, and the rain began. At first it was just
an ordinary rain but before a quarter of an hour was over

it was pouring out of the sky like water over a fall. The wind heightened. It churned up the lake in twelve-foot-high waves. In shrieks and drawn-out wails it blew with such force across the deck of the schooner that no one could stand upright.

Rose crept into the cabin where Susan was already crouched in a far corner murmuring prayers. Rose could not reach her because the ship pitched and yawed so furiously. She clung to the inside of the door jamb, watching terrified as the men moved about the deck, clinging to the ropes, the wheel, the bulkhead, anything that would keep them from being injured or blown overboard. She could hear their shouts but the wind was so wild and shrill she could not hear anything they said. Once Will went past the door, crawling on all fours, and she heard him call out to someone, ". . . says 'reef the mainsail'!"

Seconds later the ship pitched into a deep trough and the floor of the cabin stood almost straight up in the air. Rose, Susan and anything that was not nailed down were hurled against the far wall. All Rose could see, looking straight out through the porthole, was water. The schooner hung suspended for what seemed like hours, then it righted itself. In a momentary lull in the tempest, Rose heard the captain shout, "Let out the sail!" then the wind howled and the ship heeled over again.

"Susan," Rose cried, though Susan could not hear her, "did we go all that way and find Will just so we could die when we're almost home? Aunt Nan! Will! I don't want to die!" Then she stopped thinking about dying because, as the schooner righted itself once more, she was violently sick to her stomach. Three more times the ship pitched, until it nearly flipped over. Three more times it righted itself. Then, as suddenly as it had blown up, the gale was over. The wind veered straight around to the west, and steadied. But the rain went on. In sheets and torrents it poured over them. Will came in and lit the coal stove that had gone out during the gale. Susan made coffee. Rose took buckets and washed herself and the floor where she had been sick. While one man took the watch and another the wheel, the captain came into the cabin to warm himself by the stove. He said quietly, "Well, I think we might better offer up a small prayer. It was just a week ago to-day the *Laurie Jack* and all hands went down within a mile of the dock at Soames."

It was not more than fifteen minutes later when Jim Bedell, who was on watch, shouted, "I see a light," and Will said, barely containing the excitement and relief in his voice, "That'd be Soames." It wasn't ten more minutes before he said, in those same tones, "I expect that light's Arn Colliver's place." Captain Pierson shouted "Hard down! Hard down!" and the schooner headed into the bay. It sailed past Heaton's dock where Rose and Susan had embarked for Oswego only weeks earlier, past their own house and docked at the head of the bay.

"You might better stay the night with us," Jake Pierson said to Will. It was still raining hard and the wind, while it was no longer a gale, was powerful. Night had fallen while they had wrestled out on the lake.

Rose peered anxiously into the dark and the rain. She was more afraid than ever that something was about to wrong.

"Please, Will," she said, "let's go now. It's all right for you and Susan. You're home. But it isn't all right for me. Please."

Will took one look at her frightened face. "O.K. We'll go. It's only a mile and a quarter. Susan, you stay here. I'll go up the road with Rose. You come along in the morning when the rain ain't so fierce."

"I'm coming," said Susan. "Rose come along with me every step of the way to find you and I aim to come along with Rose."

Rose smiled gratefully at Susan, but Jake Pierson shook his head warningly at them.

"Bad night," he said. "Black as the inside of a cat and wet as Niagara."

Jake Pierson was right. It was black. There were no shapes of houses or barns to guide them. With Will in the lead they put their heads down against the onrushing wind and the stinging rain and marched along as fast as they could, their boots full of water, their clothes heavy and clinging.

"I wish I had my jeans," thought Rose. She pulled the long skirt away from her legs, rolled it up around her waist and held it there.

"I hear the creek." Will's voice was raised against the wind, but it sounded relieved. "I know where we are now, just about to our bridge." They went on about twenty paces when Rose heard a thrashing around as if someone had fallen. Will swore, then he shouted, "Stop! Don't come on, the bridge's washed out!" Susan grabbed her hand and they stopped.

"You all right, Will?" cried Susan.

"Yep," came Will's voice as he suddenly loomed over them. "But I don't know how we're going to get across

that water without we can even see. I don't remember
the creek ever flooding like this. There's no sign of the
bridge at all, not one stick. She's gone and the water's
like a millrace. It's up higher than my waist and rushing
so fast it pulled me right over. Standing in it, I couldn't
tell which way was east nor which was west. It's only
by your voices I knew to come this way. We're going to
have to go back. There ain't no other way we can get to
the house and the root cellar except over the creek —
and that's too dangerous.''.

''I'm not going back.'' Rose was desperate. ''You go.
I'm not going. I can swim. I'll get across. I have to!''

''We ain't leaving you,'' said Susan.

''Wait here then,'' said Will. ''I'll try again.''

''Let me come.''

''Nope.''

Rose waited. Over the sounds of the wind and the rain
she heard Will splashing. In a few moments, he was
back.

''It'd be up over your head and you couldn't ever
swim. If you climb on my back and hang on tight I think
I can get you across.''

Will squatted down and Rose hitched up her wet
skirts again and climbed up to sit on his back.

''Hang on tight,'' he shouted. Will slipped and
stumbled across the rocky creek bed, the wind and rain
pushing against him. Rose clung desperately around his
neck. Once they nearly fell but his feet found the other
side and he knelt down to let Rose off to clamber up the
slippery bank while he went back to get Susan.

It seemed to Rose that she was waiting forever. When
they reached her side, she took their hands and together

they fought the wind. It was a walk that would have taken three minutes on a calm day. It took them twenty — an agony of time for Rose. She couldn't tell when they had reached the front yard of the Morrissays' house.

But Will could. "Here we are," he said. There was quiet jubilation in his voice.

They turned into the yard and inched their way around to the back, feeling for the back porch, the stone walk, and the root cellar.

"I think I found the creek," said Will, "my foot's struck water." He stumbled and let go of Rose and Susan's hands to right himself.

"No, it ain't, this here's the creek." Susan was down on her hands and knees. "I can feel the old hawthorn tree and I know the creek goes in this direction from it."

"So what've I got my foot in?" demanded Will irritably.

"It's the root cellar," cried Rose. "It's the root cellar, and it's full of water." And she grabbed Will's hand, put her foot forward, nearly fell, pulled back, put her foot forward more cautiously, and felt around until she found a step.

"It *is* the root cellar!" she gasped. Without another word, without really thinking about what she was doing, her feet groped for the slippery steps. She held her nose and pushed herself down under the muddy water, grabbing at vines and weeds with her hands, until her feet found the floor. She stood there for as long as she could hold her breath, grasping at the edge of the steps for something to cling to, then she rose to the surface. "Oh, please," she thought desperately, "let it happen."

It was still dark, still pouring rain, the wind was still howling. It hadn't worked. She was not home.

Her disappointment was so intense she nearly fainted. She climbed up from the last step and reached out for Will or Susan for support.

"Will?" she said faintly. "Susan?"

"Is that you, Rose?" It was Sam's voice. "Where are you? You shouldn't stay out in a storm like this. It's awful."

"It is an awful storm, Sam," said Rose shakily. "But I'm all right now."

HOME

Rose stood in front of the fire, her teeth chattering, her heart thumping, streams of muddy water dripping from Louisa Jerue's green and white striped dress.

Sam stared at her. "How come you've got on that funny dress? And you're purple with cold."

"I don't think you'd believe me if I told you."

"I might."

"Do you want to hear?"

"Sure. Do you want some tea or something?"

"Yes! And a grilled cheese sandwich and a bath. What time is it?"

"Eight o'clock."

"Is it today Aunt Nan had the accident?"

"Yes, today." Sam's eyebrows went up.

"Today!" The word sounded like a sigh as Rose trailed upstairs in her dripping clothes. Twenty minutes later, warm and dry in her pajamas and bathrobe, she sat at the kitchen table drinking tea and eating sandwiches while Grimalkin purred in her lap. She told Sam all that had happened. "And Sam," she finished, "while I was in that station in New York I saw you. You were in the kitchen playing Will's song."

228   THE ROOT CELLAR

"But I did that!" Sam was incredulous. "I did that a little while ago before the twins went to bed. They were grizzling so I sat them down and I played that song, and I hate to say it because it makes it look as if I really believe your story, but in my mind I saw your face and you were scared so I was sort of playing for you to hear."

"I was glad."

"I don't know." Sam scratched his head. "It sounds crazy but you *look* different. You really look as if you've been out in the sun for weeks and" — he grinned — "you don't look as much as if you'd like to throw things at everybody. You're different."

"I am," said Rose, "I know I am. Sam, does your mother hate me?"

"Hate you?"

"Because of the accident and because I was so mean."

"I don't think my mother ever hates people. She gets mad. She says a lot of things but it doesn't last long. It's not like hating people."

"Can I go see her?"

"Why not?"

Nervously Rose knocked on the open door of Aunt Nan's bedroom. Uncle Bob was reading aloud from a novel. He looked up, obviously relieved to be interrupted.

"Come in, come in." He put down his book. "I'll go make some tea and leave you two to gab." He left the room quietly.

Rose did not want him to go. She did not want to be left alone with Aunt Nan. She felt so different from the angry little girl who had written the letter to Aunt Millicent. She couldn't think of anything to say. And for once, it seemed, Aunt Nan had nothing to say either.

Finally Rose blurted out, "I am sorry about the accident and the letter."

"I don't think it was altogether your fault." Aunt Nan smiled ruefully. "I think I had something to do with it too, Rose. I was foolish and unkind."

"I shouldn't have written the letter."

"I shouldn't have made you feel so unwelcome."

"But you didn't!"

"It's all right, Rose." Aunt Nan put out her hand. Rose went over to the bed and shook the outstretched hand. Aunt Nan held it tightly for a moment. She smiled. "I hope now we're going to take time to get to know each other."

"Yes, please."

They said goodnight and Rose went upstairs to bed, and to sleep at once. She was wakened in the night by a loud crash. Everyone except Aunt Nan — who kept calling, "What happened? What happened?" — ran to the windows to see what it was. George got the flashlight and went out to the back porch. "Wow!" he yelled, running back into the house, "There's a huge tree down, back there, and the rain has turned to ice and it's really amazing! You know if the length of that tree is any indication of ——"

"Not now, George," said Sam.

"Thank God it didn't hit the house," said Uncle Bob.

"Hi, Rose, where did you go?" asked the twins.

"Out," said Rose. She took their hands and led them upstairs to bed.

The storm had stopped by morning. The front yard was littered with branches that had come down in the night. At the back the creek was roaring and the trees were sheathed in ice, glittering in the bright sun, creaking in the slight breeze.

Rose looked down from her window. The big old maple had fallen from the other side of the creek across the glade, coming to rest not two feet from the back of the house. In its path it had knocked down bushes and uprooted several small trees. Among them was the little thorn tree. The root cellar was completely washed out. It was just a large hole filled with dirty, icy water. Its doors had been smashed by the falling tree. Rose stared down at the devastation in stunned silence. Then she raced downstairs and outside in her pajamas and bare feet. She slipped and slid and crawled over the huge icy trunk of the old maple to reach the little thorn tree. She knelt down beside it, and tenderly, as though it had been a person, she tried to lift it. It was impossible. It was lying with its branches across what had been the cellar, its roots sticking out in a tangle in all directions like the hair of some giant wild man. She felt as though a part of herself had been wrenched from her.

"I can't ever go back," she whispered.

Sam's voice behind her asked, "Is that your tree?"

"Yes." Rose clenched her fists so tightly that her nails made deep red marks in her palms. "I didn't even say goodbye," she said dully. "I didn't say anything. I just went."

Sam didn't speak but they went back into the house together. Rose went to wash Louisa's dress — as much with tears as with water. "I never thought I'd never see them again,'' she mourned, but even as the words formed she knew that she had known. At the back of her mind she had known all the way home from Washington. ''I wish I'd said goodbye,'' she whispered sadly.

That day Uncle Bob organized the house and Rose had no time for grieving. He rearranged the pots and pans in the kitchen. He started a master grocery list so that he would not have to figure out a new one every time he went to the store. He made a work list so that everyone would know exactly what his, or her — he looked meaningfully at Rose — job was without being told. As Sam said sometime later in the day, ''He'd organize our dreams if he could find out what they were.'' And all the time Uncle Bob was making lists at the kitchen table, Aunt Nan was shouting orders from the bedroom. Finally, Uncle Bob rebelled. ''Your job,'' he pronounced, ''is to lie still and sleep and rest. The house is outside your jurisdiction from now until the baby's born. Understand?''

''Yes,'' said Aunt Nan meekly.

But in the following week, everyone was surprised to discover that Aunt Nan, despite her apparent disorder, had been running things in a regulated fashion, and there was a good deal of argument and confusion despite Uncle Bob's lists.

Rose stayed out of the arguments. She went to school. She did the things beside her name on the lists. She told stories to the twins and she tried valiantly to spend her days in the present while dreams of the past filled her nights. She dreamed of coal dust and trains, of tramping the roads, of Peter Maas and Augustus Delfinney. She dreamed of pale soldiers and rows of hospital beds. She dreamed of Will and Susan — always of Susan. She missed her sorely. She could not bring herself to make friends at school, not yet.

One afternoon she got a pencil and paper and went into Aunt Nan's bedroom. "Would you like me to write down your book for you?"

Aunt Nan's face broke out in a broad smile. She told Rose where to find the chapters and notes. At first they were both self-conscious about the work, but as the afternoon progressed they began to get used to each other. Aunt Nan did most of the talking — about the book at first, but afterwards about the baby to come, about the boys and Uncle Bob, and about Christmas which was only two weeks away.

"How I hate being in bed with Christmas coming." She sighed impatiently. "Dr. Best says I'm to be allowed in a wheel chair for Christmas dinner but I can't do a thing to get it all ready. And the kitchen in this house is such a perfect Christmas kitchen. I love Christmas. Well, this year we're having a baby for Christmas even if it isn't due until January. And getting this book done is a wonderful present. I have to thank you for that, Rose."

Privately Rose thought the story, which was called *Polly Learns to Ride*, was silly, and sometimes, unbeknownst to Aunt Nan, she changed a few lines.

One afternoon, when she read out what they had written the day before, Aunt Nan said, "I like the way that scene goes. I don't even remember writing it."

"I put that in."

"You did what!" Aunt Nan nearly jumped out of bed. "Don't you dare rewrite my story!"

Rose went white. "Well, it's better. You said so yourself."

They glared at each other angrily. Then to Rose's consternation, Aunt Nan's eyes filled with tears.

Rose was stunned. "I'm sorry," she mumbled.

"It's just that you're so like your father." Aunt Nan shook her head. "How angry he used to make me! I'd make something, and if it wasn't just the way he thought it should be, he'd change it. 'Well, it's better this way, Nan,' he'd say. He was just as prickly and difficult as you are."

And as you, Rose thought to herself, and almost laughed out loud with sudden delight. She did not tell Aunt Nan she had once thought she had come from another world, without having had a mother or father, but she thought about it a lot over the next few days. And about what Will had said in the orchard about belonging. The words "as prickly and difficult as you are" had somehow brought her into Aunt Nan's family.

"And it's Christmas," she remembered. "They love Christmas here. I wish I could find something truly amazing to do for Christmas."

THE CHRISTMAS KITCHEN

One afternoon, about a week before Christmas, Rose was alone in the kitchen. She was sitting in the old rocking-chair by the window thinking that Aunt Nan was right: with its low ceiling, its wooden walls and its old fireplace, the kitchen looked like a picture on a Christmas card. She was wondering idly how many people had cooked their Christmas dinners in the fireplace, when an eddy of wind came down the chimney and curled itself around the charred ends of wood in the grate. It stirred up a tiny flame. The flame took on a shadow which became a bigger flame and, in seconds, there was a roaring fire from two steadily burning logs. A huge black pot hung over them and out of the pot steam was rising, carrying the most delicious spicy odours out into the room.

Little by little, as if in a magic show, the room changed. Along the back wall, instead of Aunt Nan's modern range, there was an old-fashioned black wood stove. Pots were hanging from hooks on the walls, and onions and dried apples and chunks of bacon were suspended from the ceiling. A tall Welsh dresser, with blue and white plates arrayed on its shelves, stood beside the front door, and there was a long, scrubbed wooden table in the middle of the room. Then Susan appeared, humming to herself as she rolled out dough with a large, wooden rolling-pin.

Rose sprang from her chair. The scene faded and she was alone again, the little eddy of wind stirring the ashes in the cold grate. She slumped back into her chair.

"Susan," she whispered, "it's true, being a person is very hard." And she heard, like an echo in her head, "that's so, Rose," and could not help smiling.

With a sigh, she went over and made a fire in the fireplace and then began to set the table, the image of Susan bright in her mind. An idea was forming.

At dinner she announced that she was going to make an old-fashioned Christmas dinner, as her present to the whole family.

"Can you cook?" the twins asked.

"Of course," she said. She knew how to cook sausages, mashed potatoes, French toast, and cabbage salad. On the rare occasions when her grandmother and she had been in their apartment in New York, if her grandmother had gone out on the maid's night out, Rose had been allowed to make dinner for herself. She had learned how to make the meals she liked best. She didn't think cooking anything could be all that difficult. After all, she reasoned, I learned to be a blacksmith and nothing in the world could be harder than that.

George was outraged. Uncle Bob was dubious, Aunt Nan thought it was a fine idea.

"Why don't you go down and talk to old Tom Bother. I'll bet he can remember old-fashioned Christmases. And ask him to come and share it with us."

Rose did not think Old Tom's memory would go back far enough for what she needed. So she asked him if he had a cookbook from his mother.

Old Tom climbed up to his attic, rummaged around and came down with two — his mother's and his grandmother's.

Rose immediately picked up his grandmother's book — dated 1857. "That's what I want!" She was delighted. She invited Old Tom for Christmas dinner and took the cookbook home.

To her dismay, most of the Christmas recipes were for game birds with rich sauces concocted from ingredients measured in scant teacups, and pats of butter the size of an acorn or a thumb. There were six recipes for chestnut soup, three for calves' foot jelly and fourteen for oyster dishes. Rose took the book back to Old Tom and together they chose a menu of things that did not appear too difficult to make and that the book assured them "all the best households" would include.

Old Tom said he would buy the goose as his present for the family. Rose was going to get the potatoes, tomatoes, onions and cranberries, and the things Old Tom called trimmings. As the book said mincemeat took a month to "ripen", she decided to buy that, but she was determined to do the rest of the baking herself.

Uncle Bob remade his lists so that Rose's name was beside dinner every night. "Need the practice," he told her. After four days George rebelled. "Last night we had sausages and mashed potatoes and cabbage salad." He pounded his fist on the table. "That means tonight we're having French toast and bacon and cabbage salad. Tomorrow we're going to have sausages and mashed potatoes and the next night French toast. I know what we're going to have for Christmas, and I don't want sausages and mashed potatoes and cabbage salad for Christmas dinner.''

''You'll see,'' was all Rose said. But the baking was not going well. Every night after dinner Rose sent everyone from the kitchen so that her pies and cakes would come as a surprise. She measured and mixed everything carefully, but pie dough (for the bought mincemeat) was not as easy to roll as Susan had made it appear. Nor was shortbread as simple as the recipe suggested. It was sticky and went into holes and lumps faster than the rolling pin could smooth it out. The expensive ingredients for plum pudding were stuck together into a thing that looked like a ball of cement with pebbles in it. Rose hoped fervently that Uncle Bob's brandy sauces would soften it up.

The day before Christmas, Uncle Bob and the boys went out to the woods and brought home a spruce tree smelling of fresh snow and winter. It fitted perfectly into the corner of the kitchen by the fireplace. Rose and the boys decorated it with St. Nicholas bells, bright balls and little shining figures that came out of the old wooden box from the attic. Rose had never trimmed a Christmas tree before. Her grandmother had only had a small, artificial silver one for the table.

''Here,'' Sam handed Rose two china cherubs. ''Mom said they belonged on our great-grandmother's tree so that's your great-grandmother, too. You put them on.'' Rose hung them carefully on the ends of branches where they could be easily seen.

After lunch the neighbours came in — Mrs. Yardly

from across the bay with candies, Mrs. Heaton from down the road with a big red and white cake, three Colliver children with cookies. They had all heard Aunt Nan was sick. Their warm generosity made Rose think of Min Jerue.

On Christmas Eve Rose put the presents she had bought under the tree. On Christmas morning she was up even before the twins. She had a book on fishing for Uncle Bob, kaleidoscopes for the twins, a deck of cards for George. She had found a wooden recorder in an antique shop in Soames for Sam. Her present for Aunt Nan was to be the kitchen all decorated for Christmas and, of course, the old-fashioned dinner. There was no light outside, although the blackness of night had softened and the stars had become dim. A sliver of moon stood over the old maple trees and there was in the air that sense of quiet expectation that lies over the land just before dawn, and that always seems so much stronger in midwinter. Rose sat down in the rocking-chair with her hands in her lap. She kept a stillness inside her, feeling that expectation, feeling, before she could see it, the dawn edge over the horizon, then reach across the earth towards the window where she sat. She felt happy and at home.

The twins got up and Christmas began. They took their stockings down from over the fireplace and crowed delightedly over every treasure they brought forth, then they went to wake Sam and George and everyone went into Aunt Nan and Uncle Bob's room.

In Rose's stocking, along with an assortment of small treats and the apple and orange and nuts everyone had, there was a miniature toy car. Some of the paint had worn off and it looked old. When Rose looked up and caught Aunt Nan's anxious expression she knew it must have belonged to her father, and she put it carefully into the pocket of her bathrobe and kept her hand tightly around it.

Then everyone opened their presents. George had bought Rose a trick bar of soap that squirted water, the twins had made her a scrapbook with pages for her to write down their favourite stories in, Aunt Nan and Uncle Bob had given her a warm sweater and an apron with Christmas wreaths and bells printed on it and Sam had found an old copy of *The Secret Garden*. Rose smiled tremulously when she said thank you to Sam but she was happier still when she saw how he liked the recorder. He played Will's song and although it made her sad, she felt right about it.

They went to church in the morning. After a small lunch, Rose shooed them all out of the kitchen. She put on Louisa Jerue's carefully washed and ironed, green and white striped dress, and over it her new Christmas apron.

Then she decorated the kitchen. Uncle Bob had saved some small spruce branches for her and she put them in a glass dish in the centre of the table on Aunt Nan's printed, holly-wreath table cloth. She put out the big Christmas paper napkins, the good wine glasses and dishes. It felt to her like a wonderful game, and she was full of excitement.

The green of the spruce, the bright cloth, the twinkling lights of the tree, and the glow from the fireplace, made the room look something like the old-fashioned Christmas pictures she wanted to conjure up.

"So what I have to do now is get the dinner," she told Grimalkin who was prowling and sniffing around the edges of his suddenly unfamiliar kitchen.

As she said it she became aware that possibly everyone who had ever lived in the house was making Christmas dinner. Pots clattered, dishes rattled, there was talk and laughter in cloud-like layers that moved together, separated, piled up, dispersed again. And there were odours, rich, inviting odours from how many years of how many Christmases!

With a blissful sense of being a part of all those other festivities, Rose peeled potatoes and got them ready, sweet ones and white, according to the recipe in *Home Cookery*. The tomatoes were in a tin and only needed a few spices to make them right. She skinned the onions and made a cream sauce. "A little lumpy" — she tasted it — "but not bad. I knew I could do this!" She took the goose out of the refrigerator and opened Aunt Nan's cookbook. As she was using a modern oven, Old Tom had suggested a modern cookbook for the goose.

"Roast goose," said the book, "twenty to twenty-five minutes to the pound." She read no farther. It was four o'clock. The goose weighed ten pounds.

"I never thought about the time!" Rose gulped. "Well, I'll have to cook it hotter than it says. Then it will go faster." She stuffed it with apples and onions, turned the oven temperature as high as it would go and shoved in the goose.

Within five minutes, Rose's goose was as aromatic as all the Christmas dinners in all those other times. Within three more minutes it had started to burn. She yanked open the oven door and pulled it out. It was black on top.

"Rose, Rose, how long is it to dinner?" The twins breathed through the keyhole.

"Not yet," Rose's voice quavered. "Go away. All of you," she called.

"I know," she sighed with relief, "you have to heat the oven first." She sat down and waited until the temperature said 500 degrees then shot the goose back in the oven.

This time it was almost fifteen minutes before the smell of burning goose was strong. Rose jerked the roasting pan out of the oven with such force that she sat down on the floor with it in her lap. There was a great red burn on her arm, and grease on her Christmas apron and her dress.

"It isn't going to cook," she said in a low hoarse voice. "And the potatoes and things are almost cold. It's ruined." After all that she had been through with Will and Susan, a ruined dinner might not have seemed very important. But all Rose's longing to be a part of the family had centred on it, and she was sick with disappointment.

Old Tom arrived at the front door.

"Rose, shall I get Aunt Nan settled in the wheel chair?"

"No! No! Give me fifteen minutes."

She picked the cat away from the goose. "No Grimalkin." She swallowed hard. "That's Boxing Day dinner. Today we're going to have sausages and mashed potatoes and cabbage salad." She imagined George's face as he saw what was for Christmas dinner.

"You can get ready, now," she called. She felt much as she had the time she had made up her mind to work for Peter Maas. She went about her work with that same fatalistic calm. She put on a clean apron, she wrapped up the goose and put it back in the refrigerator. She put sausages on to cook and mashed the potatoes.

She ran to the cupboard and took down the tins full of rock-hard cookies and skimmed them out the back door like flat stones into a lake.

"Merry Christmas rabbits and squirrels and chickadees," she whispered.

She piled the sausages on the big turkey platter, with the mashed potatoes beside them. "They're going to hate me for this," she murmured. She walked slowly towards the door, opened it, slid through, and stood with her back to it as though she were protecting a hidden spy.

Everyone clustered around her, Uncle Bob pushing Aunt Nan in the wheel chair.

"Rose, you look like a Christmas picture!" cried Aunt Nan. "Where did you get that wonderful dress?"

Rose did not answer. She looked at Aunt Nan with pleading eyes. Resolutely she smiled.

"Well now," said Old Tom, "this promises to be quite a surprise." He winked at Rose.

"Yes, it does." She bit her lip. "Well, merry Christmas everybody." She threw open the kitchen door.

For at least a minute there was not a sound. In the soft glow of the firelight and candles the astonished gathering saw a room so bedecked and garlanded with cedar and pine it looked like a fairytale forest. On the mantelpiece, branches of green were twisted around a pair of creamy white candles in tall candlesticks that Rose had never seen before. On the table in front of the window were lighted oil lamps. The dinner table was covered with a soft white linen cloth embroidered with wreaths in rose and green silk. At every place there were linen napkins that matched, and white plates with thin, green and rose flowered rims. The wine glasses were cranberry coloured. In the centre of the table candles in pewter candlesticks were circled by a wreath of cedar.

A large platter stood at the serving end of the table and on it was a roast goose, brown and glossy. And there were covered serving dishes and relishes and pickles and hot bread and jellies.

Old Tom broke the silence. "You mean to tell me that little girl done all this?" Then everyone began to talk at once and their words were a jumble and a buzz in Rose's head all through dinner. She ate, got up, cleared away the plates and brought over the candles and the dessert, a plump Christmas pudding which had been sitting on a trivet by the hearth. Only then did she begin to think. Had Susan brought it all? Had she made it all? Or had she spent the day swiping it from a hundred and fifty years of other people's Christmases? Had she had to eat sausages and mashed potatoes for Christmas dinner?

Uncle Bob stood up and dinged his glass with his spoon. "Ladies and gentlemen," he said. "In the forces, at formal dinners, there are toasts to distinguished members of the company. On this occasion I feel sure there can be no argument that my niece, Rose Larkin, is the most distinguished member of this company. I'd like to propose the first toast to Rose, a young woman who performs miracles and understands Christmas. To Rose." Uncle Bob lifted his glass.

"To Rose." Aunt Nan smiled at her.

"And God bless," said Old Tom. Self-consciously the boys followed suit.

Rose looked at Sam then at Aunt Nan. "It wasn't me," she said. "It was Susan. That one I made was awful. The goose burned and I made sausages."

"I told you I smelled sausages," George interrupted.

Rose continued. "I think I'd better tell you about it." Once again she told her story. Then she got up and took the burned goose out of the refrigerator.

No one said a word. Uncle Bob cleared his throat a few times. George, to Rose's great delight, looked flabbergasted. Finally the twins said, "Tell again about the girl in our room." Aunt Nan said thoughtfully, "There's Sam's ghost," and subsided into silence. Sam took his recorder out of his pocket. He leaned over to Rose and said softly, "I think I would have liked Will." And Rose said, "Oh, Sam, you would have."

Old Tom, who had said very little all evening, nodded his head. "You remember, youngster, I told you about old Susan Morrissay living in this house and how her nephew used to come summers. I never saw no ghosts here but there's been talk about this place. Heatons used to try to keep hired men here but there wasn't none who'd stay."

"I'd like some more coffee." Uncle Bob held out his cup. When it came he lifted it to his lips and quickly put it down, the expression on his face saying plainly that he had suddenly realized where it might have come from. Everyone laughed and the spell was broken. Uncle Bob decided that no matter what they said, Rose and Old Tom had cooked up the story with the dinner, and

George agreed with him. Aunt Nan was quiet and Rose knew, from having spent so many afternoons with her, that she was figuring out how to make the story into chapters.

When the last crumb of the maple sugar candies had disappeared, Rose announced, "They're my ghosts. My friends. I'm going to do the dishes."

Uncle Bob argued but Rose was determined. Once more she closed the kitchen door after them. Quietly and carefully she washed the old plates and glasses, folded up the napkins and the cloth. When she was finished she stood in front of the dying fire. "Susan, where will I put them so that you can get them again?"

It wasn't from in front of the fire but from the old rocking-chair by the window that the voice came, and it wasn't Susan's, it was Mrs. Morrissay's. "Just leave them on the table."

Rose turned and faced her. "It was your present! I thought it was Susan's. I really thought . . . ." As she said it she could hear Old Tom's words in her head, words she hadn't really heard when he had said them. "Old Susan Morrissay."

"Susan's me," said Mrs. Morrissay.

"Susan?" said Rose doubtfully.

"That's so," said Susan. Rose walked slowly over to where she sat in the chair, old and white haired, her eyes as bright and black as they had been at fourteen.

"But this isn't — I mean wasn't — your house. It was Will's mother's."

"Rose, didn't you figure? Will and me got married. After his ma died it was our house, Will's and mine. I always loved this house." She stroked the old wood of the window sill. "Then, after Will died, I lived here alone for a lot of years."

"Did Will die soon? Did he die soon after we came back?"

"Oh, mercy no! He lived to be a good sixty years. He never did take to farming." Susan laughed. "But we always made out all right. Will stayed with the flute and he took to fiddling. He used to fiddle for all the dances hereabouts. He swore this place wasn't going to be so glum after his mother died and it never was. It was full of music. We never had no children — none that lived. We had a little girl." Susan reached out for Rose's hand. "We called her Rose, but she only lived a few weeks. We never had another. But we always had children around. We had a good life. I'm almost ninety now and it seems a long time ago."

"But you don't forget?"

"Mercy no! I don't forget them good years and I don't forget the times we had together, you and me." Susan smiled, and in the smile Rose saw her Susan, and they were setting out again in the early morning to get on a schooner to take them across Lake Ontario to find Will.

"I won't forget either, Susan." Rose sat down on the floor beside the rocking-chair.

"I got your silver rose yet." Susan reached up and slowly undid the chain from around her neck. "It's been good luck to me. I guess it's time now to give it back."

Rose fastened the chain once more around her own neck. They fell silent, smiling at each other. Rose got up and leaned over and kissed Susan's old, wrinkled cheek.

A feeling of peace came over her. Susan smiled again. Then she disappeared.

Rose looked down at the chair where Susan had been sitting. Then she sat down in it and began to rock, thinking, remembering.

"I loved this house," Susan had said. "So do I," whispered Rose, and in those words were a promise. She would see to it that the house was made right. She would bully and cajole the rest of the family into repairing and painting. She would make the garden beautiful in the spring, and get Uncle Bob to plant an orchard where there had been one in 1865 when Will Morrissay had gone off to war.

She knew in her heart that she would never see Susan again, nor Will. But, in the years that followed, Rose thought she saw shadows, and often she felt their presence — especially in the spring when the lilacs and the apples were in blossom.

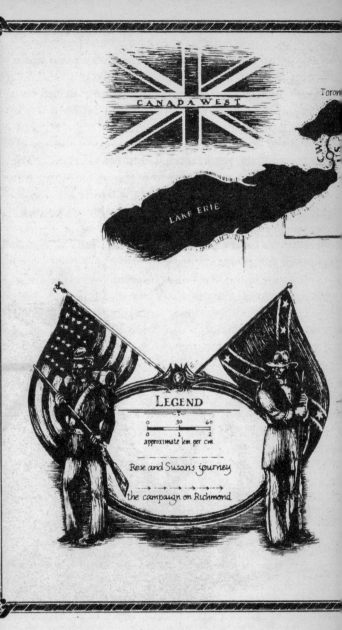

CANADA WEST

Toron

C.W.

LAKE ERIE

LEGEND

0   30   60
0   1   2
approximate km. per cm.

Rose and Susans journey

the campaign on Richmond

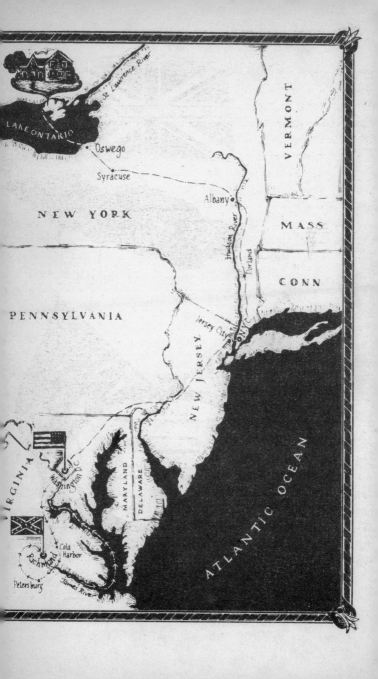